I, Judas

Jason Serbu

This book is a work of fiction. All characters and events portrayed in this book are either fictitious or are used fictitiously.

I, Judas

Front Cover photo, "Arc of the Ancient Carsulae in Infrared," by Dscmax, available on www.dreamstime.com

Back Cover photo of author by Holly Sanford Photography
http://hsphotography.zenfolio.com/
Used with permission.

Merriweather Editions
Denver

ISBN: 0615464769
ISBN-13: 978-0615464763

For Donna, Flurry and Chloe, with all my love.

A special thanks to Damon Talabock and Cathy Manning for their help and encouragement on this book.

Chapter One

"We found the safe."

Judas nodded his approval to Slava. The frightened couple, huddled together across from Judas, turned at the sound of the thick Russian accent to see a large man standing behind them. Slava placed a heavy hand upon each of their shoulders, bidding them to keep still.

"Mr. Davenport," Judas called, snapping his fingers impatiently, "the safe?"

The old man turned slowly back to face Judas, eyes wide with fear. Based on his reaction, Judas figured that there must be large sums, perhaps enough to make a difference to a great many people, but he himself cared not for earthly riches.

1

Judas leaned in closer, his attention rapt on his mark and the much younger wife seated next to him. An expansive marble coffee table, large enough to seat a family at dinner in less affluent communities, lay between them. Behind the couple, Slava stood at attention, pistol at his side; ready should Judas need him.

The wife almost conjoined herself to her husband; one arm around his neck, another around his sizeable stomach. Yet there was a definite distinction of bodies; the silhouette of her slim, toned, augmented body could never be mistaken for the older, shapeless, corpulent form of her husband. She also differed in that she held a more defiant stare, in sharp contrast to her husband's fading stubbornness. She was defending something far more precious than the contents of her husband's safe.

"Mr. Davenport," Judas said, sliding to the edge of his seat, a difficult task considering the degree of incline to the expensive designer chair in which he sat, "would you be so kind as to give me the combination to your safe?"

"You go to hell."

"Please sir, we're in mixed company," Judas replied.

He then motioned to Slava, who disappeared from the room only to return minutes later pushing a young boy in a wheelchair. The child sat motionless, unaware of his surroundings; his life sustained by the many wires that tethered him to a machine.

"You leave him be," the wife screamed, as she leapt to her feet, only to freeze as Slava pulled out his gun and leveled it at her head.

"Please, Slava, that is not necessary. We are guests in the Davenport's home and we should act accordingly."

"You're trespassers and thieves and you are not welcome here," Mr. Davenport managed, despite a wavering voice.

2

"I think you will find, upon our departure that we were most welcome and you will forever look back upon this day as one of your most fortunate. Now please, Mrs. Davenport, won't you sit down?"

She tried to appear calm as she sat, but the trembling of her lower jaw betrayed her. She felt the fear rising as she watched Judas' gaze move over her child. She noticed with a rising sense of horror that he was smiling as he approached the boy. With bated breath he caressed the menagerie of wires that controlled his breathing, heart rate and waste functions.

"How old is he?" Judas inquired.

"Monster," she screamed.

"Ma'am, please, what do you take me for?"

"A thief and a murderer," she replied.

"I've committed no murder. And I am no thief, as I have not taken anything. All I want is the contents of your safe, but you will give them to me willingly. I hardly call that the act of a thief."

"You'll kill us after you get what you're after!"

"Please," Davenport began, trying to calm his wife, "please don't upset them."

"Then do something," she demanded of her husband.

"They have guns," he whispered meekly.

"Yes, we have guns, but we have never, ever had to use them. We do not persuade with force. You will find our methods are far more agreeable than that."

"Just sit tight and do as they say," the husband said to his wife.

"You should listen to your husband. A man doesn't get to where he is without hard work. And he certainly doesn't acquire this kind of wealth," Judas said as he waved his arms around, "without sacrifice."

3

Judas studied them both for a moment, and then moved even closer to the boy.

"Get away from him!" Mrs. Davenport screamed.

He paused, smiled at the woman, and turned his attention back the young boy.

"How old is he?"

"Se, seven. He's seven," Mr. Davenport said.

"And he's always been like this?"

"Please leave him alone. Take what you want, but please don't hurt him," said Mrs. Davenport, her commanding voice now surrendered to the fear of possible harm coming to her son.

"May I have the combination to the safe?" Judas asked.

"Please, don't hurt us," the old man begged.

"We don't want to hurt you, we want to help you," Judas began, "but in order to do that, we need the combination to your safe. May I please have it?"

Judas reached down and lightly placed his fingers on the tube connecting Peter's lungs to the machine's monitor. He lingered there, then continued to the monitor, then along the wires and then his fingers finally came to rest at the straps that held the boy captive to the chair.

He took hold of the strap that held his legs and with a quick motion, flicked it away, leaving the boy's stick legs dangling from the chair.

"No," they both screamed but they did not move.

He ignored them as they continued their pleas. He worked in an indulgent fashion as he freed the child's body, leaving it attached only to the machinery keeping him alive. He bent down, and with little effort, lifted up the child.

"Mr. Davenport. I'd really appreciate it if you'd give me the combination to your safe. You're a very wealthy man. You've done well. You have a very nice home, a bit large for my taste, but nicely furnished, obviously by your wife, or more accurately, by someone she's hired. Nice job, Mrs. Davenport. Now, to the matter at hand, you have something I want. And that is the contents of your safe. Would you please give me the combination?"

"Please, don't," Davenport said, his voice quivering as tears began to flow. He was terrified now, something a man of his position and power never felt. He struggled to keep his eyes fixed on his son, preferring not to feel the humiliation when he meet Judas' gaze.

"I'll ask you once more; please, the combination?"

Davenport's mouth opened but offered no sound. His wife's grip on him so strong it was leaving marks.

"Very well then," said Judas as he grabbed all the wires from the machine and pulled them free. A small alarm went off as the lines on the monitor flat lined.

"No!" the wife screamed. She tried to get up, but Slava's firm hand kept her seated. Mr. Davenport only wept, resigned to the inevitable conclusion at hand.

"It is not too late. Tell me the…" Judas said

"24 left, 36 right, 15 left, 13 right, zero," Mr. Davenport blurted out as he wept freely.

"Thank you. That wasn't so hard now was it?" Judas replied.

He looked up and nodded to Slava. The large man then pulled out a radio and repeated the numbers to another man who answered in a different accent. He then nodded back to Judas and left the room.

Judas looked down at the child in his arms, the life slowly leaving his emaciated body.

"You've given us a gift, what is in your safe, and I thank you. As a token of my gratitude, let me offer you something in return, something worth far more than the contents of your safe, your bank accounts, your home, worth more than everything you could ever possess."

Judas carried the child to the front of the coffee table and sat on it. He was now only a few feet from the couple. He pulled the child closer and cuddled his frail body into his chest.

He then closed his eyes and spoke to the child, whispered something that the couple could hear, but didn't understand. He then nodded and turned his attention back to the Davenports.

"Tell me, do you believe in salvation?"

They both nodded, very slowly, yet they never took their eyes from their son.

"Good. Then I have a proposition for you."

He then fell to his knees, still clutching the child, and began to convulse into spasms.

Chapter 2

Judas slept, his head resting on the shoulder of the large Russian man. Though he had not worn a mask like the others, his hair was matted and damp, lending an almost greasy reflection whenever the lampposts would intrude with their sickly light as the car sped by.

Father Donovan twisted in the passenger seat and looked back as much as the seatbelt would allow. The constriction of the belt made him aware that the others never wore seatbelts. He also noticed that none of the others paid any attention to the man in the middle of the back seat.

"Does he always do that?" Donovan asked to whoever would answer, eyes riveted to the sleeping Judas.

No one answered. In fact, as Donovan now noted, no one moved; everyone seemed a still life, frozen in their seat.

"I could never sleep after that," Donovan offered.

He turned towards Crispis, the driver, expecting an answer, but got none. He returned his gaze to the rear seat, but the men on either side of his fascination did not reply. They sat as if carved from stone. The occasional pothole that shook the car did nothing to move them. Even when the force of the jarring would send Judas' head from Slava's hard physique to Mac's soft shoulder and back again, they did not move.

Donovan tried staring down the man on either side of the sleeping man. Neither man returned his gaze. He made faces, waved his hands close to their faces; nothing, no response. It was if he wasn't there.

He turned back now, facing forward. He began to fidget with the air vent adjacent to the passenger door. He flipped it up and down, switched the lever open and closed. He did this several times, and then growing bored, leaned into the passenger door and rested his head against the glass. His eyes searched eagerly for any movement from the street outside, but it was late and nothing was to be found.

To alleviate his boredom, Donovan breathed heavily on the window, fogging it up. He then pressed his index finger on the glass and began to doodle. He breathed again on the glass, to keep the medium of his creations from disappearing, but each time after a few strokes of his fingers, the medium would disappear.

He sunk back into his seat, nervous energy abound, but now beginning to feel defeated.

"I still can't see how he does it," he remarked, this time to no one in particular.

"Do what?" Crispis replied.

The young priest rose suddenly, excitedly. He would have left his seat had the retraction of the seat belt not caught his motion and forced him back. He struggled to sit up and when he couldn't get the seat belt to slacken quickly enough, he unbuckled himself.

"How can he sleep like that after a job?" Donovan replied excitedly, almost getting too close to the driver.

Crispis studied Donovan for a full minute. He then glanced up into the rear view mirror. There he spied Mac and Slava flanking the sleeping man. Slava gazed straight ahead oblivious to the driver's stare and seemingly unaware of the man's head resting on his shoulder while Mac, stared straight ahead, remaining motionless.

"Sleep?" Crispis laughed, turning to Donovan, "Shit, he just plain passes out sometimes. Though, I doubt you can call it sleep."

"Da, goes comatose," offered Slava, in his thick Russian accent, from the backseat without meeting the gaze of the questioner.

"I can't see how he can sleep," the young priest proclaimed.

"He's been doing this longer than you've been alive," the driver said.

"Da, much, much longer," Slava added.

"I'm all freaked out. Aren't you guys excited?"

"You get used to it," the driver answered.

Donovan stared wondrously at Judas, then at the driver and finally at the other two men.

"You think he's dreaming?" he asked.

Crispis turned to him and offered only a weary expression.

"I don't know kid."

"You guys seem," the young priest began, "I don't know, like this wasn't a very big deal. I mean, that kid, in the wheelchair, he…"

Donovan looked around the car for the slightest glimmer of joy but found none. The driver no longer eyed

9

him. Having lost all interest in the subject, he resumed staring straight out at the road ahead. The men in the car, it seemed, suddenly had forgotten Donovan was in the car, had forgotten the heist that took place a short time ago and had forgotten the miracle that followed it.

A pothole bounced the car violently, again sending the man's head rolling from Slava's shoulder onto Mac's. The young priest leaned over the seat back to study Judas up close and turned back to the driver.

"Hey, he's smiling! Does it look like he's smiling to you? Yeah. He must be dreaming, huh?" he asked around the vehicle, turning from person to person, but got no response, no eye contact, nothing. "I hope it's a pleasant dream," he added before finally surrendering and turning back to look out the passenger window.

Had Donovan not given up so easily, he might have seen the smile creep up on the driver's face or the two conscious men in the rear seat meet the driver's gaze in the rearview mirror.

"At least someone's enjoying this," Donovan said quietly under his breath.

The others were not, however, enjoying this. They've done this many times, returning from their missions in the exact same manner; dead silence while the man slept. Their stoic faces masking the same worry every time.

They suspected the troubles that gnawed away inside the sleeping man's head. They suspected the burdens and the torments, but they never spoke of them. They knew from what Judas had told them, and more intimately, from how each of them had met him, and would silently acknowledge each other with eye contact. One look would suffice, would say it all. No need for winks or nods of the head.

They knew each other's stories, of how they came to be here. Mac, the oldest, knew the history, was there when

Judas found Slava. Crispis, the slender man from the Caribbean, was the youngest of the three. They knew of each other's circumstances; of the paths they had chosen, of the deeds committed, acts of charity and sin let loose upon the world. They knew why Judas had chosen them, had saved them, had offered them a second chance. What they did not know was how this young priest, a man still of the cloth, came to be counted among them.

Crispis looked over at Donovan, sulking at the window, and placed a hand on his shoulder. When Donovan turned, he was met with a warm smile. This was the first time one of them had acknowledged him, made him feel the least bit welcome.

"Let me tell you a story," Crispis began. "The year was 1959 and I was driving a taxi on Paradise Island in the Bahamas..."

Chapter 3

The rain beat heavily against the windshield, the wipers pumping furiously in a futile attempt to fight the deluge of water.

"It rains a lot in the Bahamas this time of year," the driver offered to the passenger in the back seat. "You might get one good day of sun, if you're lucky."

He looked up into the rearview and studied the man, dressed in an outfit that readied him for rain, yes, but was more likely for colder weather. The thick overcoat, collar turned up, with a scarf tucked neatly inside. The man's face was weathered, not old with lines or wrinkles, but with enough time spent in the sun.

"Good thing you don't need to work on your tan," the driver joked. He looked up into the mirror for a reaction, a smile maybe, but the man just ignored him.

"American?" the driver asked.

"Pardon," the man replied.

"I asked, are you American?"

"No."

"British, then?"

"No."

"Good," the driver replied, "the only thing the British did for us is give us short pants and tall socks."

The driver laughed at his joke and noticed the man's somber expression give way to a faint smile. He had him, the driver thought. He was always good with people, could walk into a bar and be friends with everyone by the time he left. He was jovial by nature with a kind heart.

"So, what brings you to our little slice of paradise?"

The man in the rear seat looked up and met his gaze in the mirror. He shifted a bit, loosened his scarf and sat upright. The driver thought he noticed a large scar across the man's throat, but when he looked again, it was gone.

"I'm here on holiday."

"You picked a bad time."

"Why's that?"

The driver motioned at the onslaught of water that was having its way with the windshield.

"Rainy season," he answered. "Like I said, maybe you get one day of sun, God willing."

"I like the rain."

"You got to *love* the rain!" he joked.

"What's your name?" the man asked abruptly, before the driver finished laughing.

"Crispis."

"Crispis. Crispis," the man repeated. "That's an old name."

"Don't you go thinking I didn't hear about it growing up; I was teased relentlessly"

13

"I haven't heard that name in a while."

"Most people haven't heard that name *before*," the driver joked.

"Who gave it to you?"

"My father. Him was a good man, my father, a strong man and very handsome."

"Much like yourself."

Crispis wasn't used to flattery. He wasn't used to people taking an interest in his life. He was accustomed to pulling facts from strangers, getting them to open up about their lives. He might have otherwise found it strange to be so candid with a stranger, but he felt oddly at peace, even happy. And this was something he hadn't felt in quite some time.

"Thank you," Crispis said, "but most people think I look like my mother."

"She must be very beautiful."

"You needn't flatter me such; I'm not going to drop you at a bad spot."

"Why do you say that?"

"They warn you, don't they, at the airport, about getting into taxis that are not yellow?"

"They did."

"Mine's green."

"I liked the color."

"Well, besides, white people, if you don't mind me saying, they don't find people of color attractive."

"I'm not white."

Crispis looked again in the mirror, searching for some feature on the man's face that would tell him his nationality, his race, anything.

"Well sir, you sure ain't dark like me."

"No, I guess not."

"Where are you from then?"

"All over."

"You gonna make me guess? Maybe you don't want me to know. That's ok. I apologize, I didn't mean to…"

"Let's just say my lineage is Mediterranean."

"Greek? Roman?"

"Sure, why not?"

"You're a good sport mister."

"Thank you."

"Listen," Crispis began, "we're near the address, but I don't feel too good about dropping you here."

"Why not?"

"It's not too good a neighborhood."

"It's fine."

"You sure?"

"Yes."

Crispis looked at the address one more time. There was something familiar about the house number, but he couldn't place it. He shrugged it off, then slowed the car and turned off the pavement onto a dirt road, overgrown with weeds and debris. He slowed the car to almost a crawl, weaving around crumbled bricks and tree roots, broken bottles and planks of rotten wood that he hoped didn't hide any rusted nails that would puncture his tires.

The rain began to let up to moderate downpour, just enough so that the house could be seen for what it was in the fading light. A small white washed bungalow with peeling paint. The roof had several holes in it, two windows were broken and the front door, what was left of it, was wide open.

Crispis sat ramrod straight. A chill crept down his back and he began to fight back tears that began to swell up. He knew what address this was. In an instant, all the horrors of his past came crashing upon his, washing over him like the rain, leaving him with the hopeless feeling of drowning.

15

Crispis turned to face the man, his mouth forming around words that would not come. He could hear his breathing, rapid and hoarse, but he could not feel it. He felt like he was suffocating.

"This should do," said the man.

He handed a large sum of cash to Crispis, who just sat motionless. After a few seconds, after Crispis made no motion to accept the fare, the man dropped the cash over the seat and opened the door.

"Wait!" Crispis finally managed.

"Yes?"

"This is too much," Crispis replied, without even looking at the money that lay in a large, messy pile on the passenger seat.

"I'm sure it is. Keep it."

The man adjusted his collar against the rain and was almost out the rear door when Crispis finally felt his hand reach out and grab the man's shoulder.

"Please."

"Yes?"

"I cannot drop you here."

"Why not?"

"It's a shanty."

"A shanty?"

"A shanty. A shit hole. Look at the place. It's run down. How can anyone live there?"

"Many people live in shanties. There's no shame in it."

"No, this house…bad things have happened here."

"Bad things?"

"Please let me take you away from here."

"I don't know, it does have a quiet charm."

"Listen to me!" Crispis replied in a panic, unaware that he was shouting, "We must leave now!"

16

He slammed the shifter into gear and spun the tires as he swung the car around and sped down the drive. The car lurched violently to and fro as Crispis no longer took care to avoid the debris. The man in the back held on the best he could. When Crispis looked up at him in the mirror, he found him smiling.

As they reached the road, the speed of the car caused them to bounce and slide across the wet pavement. As Crispis fought to regain control, the car finally responded as it straightened in the oncoming lane. The headlights of a large truck approaching made him attempt to put the car back in its proper lane. This time, however, his panic caused him to overshoot their lane and the car plowed into the small drainage ditch at the side of the road. The car slowed suddenly, and Crispis began sawing at the wheel and accelerating to gain traction. He thought he was about to get the vehicle on the road again when the shoulder of the ditch collapsed, forcing the front end away from the pavement and slamming it against the bank at the far side of the road.

Crispis sat shaking, hands gripping the steering wheel, knuckles almost white. He could feel his heart beating furiously in his throat and for the first time he was aware of his breathing.

The man in the back leaned forward and placed a hand on Crispis' shoulder. He said something that he could not make out. The man leaned closer and spoke loudly.

"You can take your foot off the gas, we're stuck!"

Crispis looked down and saw that his leg was straight, felt his muscles straining to keep the accelerator pressed firmly against the floor.

"Yes," he said finally, nodding in agreement and finally, he let go of the wheel and relaxed his leg.

He turned off the ignition and sat back deeply against the seat.

17

After a moment, Crispis regained his composure.

"I'm very sorry."

"Please, do not worry. That was quite a piece of driving. In fact, if the ditch hadn't crumbled on that one side, you'd have had it."

"I'm very sorry," he repeated, "we're stuck and it's my doing. Please, I don't live too far up this road. If you don't mind the walk, you may stay with me. I will carry your bags. There is an umbrella in the trunk."

"That would be fine," the man said.

After walking for twenty minutes, they approached a simple house set a car's length from the road. Crispis opened the door and ushered the man inside.

"You must be freezing," he began, "please let me take your coat. I have wonderful beverages. Please have whatever you like."

"I'll have whatever you're having."

"Very good!"

He retrieved an unmarked bottle from the small kitchen and returned with two glasses. He poured generous amounts of the liquid into each glass, and then offered one to the man.

"Here's to wealth," Crispis toasted. "May you live to be a wealthy man!"

The man took the glass, but paused as Crispis drank first. He looked him dead in the eye, then finally brought the glass up so that it obscured his line of sight, making Crispis' figure waver in the refracted light.

"Tell me, what is this?"

"This, my good friend, is an old recipe, it is…"

"No, not the drink. This."

"I do not understand," Crispis answered.

"This," the man answered, "is wealth. Not money, nor power, but fellowship. This drink provides fellowship and nothing can be of greater value."

Crispis thought for a second and agreed excitedly, although inside he felt a bit uneasy. What did this man want? He could not place his ethnicity. He could not tell if he was black or white. His accent escaped him. He seemed nonplused, maybe even happy the entire time, the entire brief time he knew him. In fact, Crispis thought, wasn't he smiling at one point, when the car was beyond his control?

He watched the man drain his glass in one swallow. He then moved across the room and refilled his glass. The two sat drinking like this, late into the night until Crispis, groggy from the drink and the bottle empty, was lost to sleep.

When he awoke, he was alone, in his bed. He rose uneasily and sat up. He reached for the nightstand and in the dark found the object he reached for every night and every morning; a picture of a young woman with an infant. The glass was cracked and the frame damaged, but it was his most prized possession. As he held it, he found himself weeping, something he had not done in some time. He remembered the evening before, remembered the fare and where it led him. He jumped from the bed and rushed into the other room, then the kitchen. No sign of the man.

Crispis stood in the darkness of the room, listening to the wind howl against the house. He felt the cold of the floor on his feet and was aware of how cool the air was, but he was not cold. What made him shiver was the sudden realization that this man maybe was not a man at all. Maybe he was a ghost. But weren't ghosts familiar? Didn't ghosts come in the guise of someone you've known? He had never seen this man before, never seen anyone like him.

He began to shake now, uncontrollably. He let the picture escape his grasp and it fell onto the hard floor and shattered. He felt again like he was choking, unable to breathe. Before tonight he had only felt that once.

That night long ago when his wife and infant child were found murdered in their home. This house, the address the man had given him, was where his world had come to an end. He had forgotten, forced himself to do so, but tonight he was there again, brought back by this man, whatever he was.

He felt ashamed for forgetting. He had to; it was too powerful, too destructive an event to live through. He knew now what had to be done, what he had put off long ago.

He reached down at the picture at his feet and pulled a long shard of glass from the wreckage. He stood straight up and drew the shard across both wrists. When he felt the blood wouldn't flow quick enough, he drew it across his throat, felt the burning sensation give way to calm.

He stood there waiting and looking down at the picture of his family, of what was once his life. He watched as the blood dripped quickly now onto the floor.

He looked up and was startled to realize that the man from the night before was standing before him. His wrists too dripped blood and exactly like his own, the man's throat was cut and blood streamed down onto his white shirt.

"Who, who," Crispis began, but his vocal chords where done in and blood crept down his throat, choking his last words.

The man reached out a hand, a hand dark and wet from blood, and stepped forward to touch Crispis.

As Crispis reached out and received his touch, he realized that his wounds were gone, his hands were dry. He reached a hand up to his throat and found it intact. He looked at the man before him, trying to stand upright against the weight of such wounds.

"I have gone by many names, out of necessity. You may know of me as Judas, Judas Iscariot," he said, "and I have a proposition for you."

He then collapsed to the floor.

***

Crispis pulled the car over in front of St. Sebastian's Cathedral. He motioned for Donovan to come closer. As he did the driver leaned in and spoke in hushed tones.

"No one is to know of him. NO ONE. Is that understood?"

Donovan nodded hesitantly; he looked back at the sleeping man. Could it really be him, he thought? No, it wasn't possible.

"But he's," Donovan began hoarsely, "he's dead. Judas died. He killed himself. It's in the, in the bible."

"Not a word," repeated the driver. "Now get out."

Donovan watched as the large sedan sped off into the night. He turned to look up at the façade of the imposing house of God at which he served. He looked at the cross at the top of the steeple. He always thought that God had plans for him. That's why he chose to become a priest. That's way, he reasoned, that he graduated seminary early, had been given his own Parish, a parish with a large congregation, money, people with power all hanging on his every word every Sunday. But this? This made him feel insignificant. He was in awe of this man. What he had witnessed tonight was a miracle.

Donovan closed his eyes, lowered his head and made the sign of the cross three times. He then entered the rectory and as soon as his head hit the pillow, he was fast asleep.

Chapter 4

Detective Deborah Eisen ran a finger along the books that stood in perfect alignment in the beautifully crafted bookcase. Not one spine stood out past the rest. She inspected her finger; no residue, no dust. She rubbed her thumb against her forefinger and began again on the next shelf. She lingered a bit as she noticed a book by Carl Jung.

"Are you a fan?"

"I've studied his work, yes," the therapist answered, shifting in his chair, the lush leather of the wingback sighing slightly.

"Are you a fan, or a disciple?"

"A disciple requires a good amount of faith. How's your faith, Deborah?"

"Detective," she corrected.

"Detective, how do you feel about that?"

She ignored him and turned her attention back to the bookcase, running her finger along another shelf. She stopped midway through, slid her finger up the spine of a book, and pulled it out.

"Sleep Cycles of the Clinically Depressed," she read aloud. "Good book?"

"Better at getting you to sleep."

"That's clever. Maybe I'll borrow it."

"Feel free," he offered.

She slid the book back into place and continued to peruse the collection, this time stepping back to admire the whole collection.

"You've got all the right books."

"Thank you."

The detective turned towards the unoccupied desk. It was adorned with the usual items that gave the hint of use, but it seemed almost decorative; as if the neatness was for show, to impart the notion that this individual was very much together, as opposed to the visitor, who was broken. Everything lined up, evenly spaced; so much symmetry. The doctor watched from across the room, making mental notes of her methods.

She nodded silently and picked up a gold plated letter opener. She felt its heft in her hands, paused for a moment and placed it back on the desk, but purposefully not in the same place and out of alignment of the other objects. She casually turned to watch his reaction, but found none.

She walked over to the chaise lounge. She lingered a bit, unsure if she wanted to sit down.

"Is this where they sit?"

"They?"

"Your patients."

"I prefer not to call them patients."

"Why not?"

"It sounds as if they are infirmed, as if a judgment has been rendered upon them."

"Hmm," she nodded, "very reasonable. And what do you call them?"

"Tom, Judy…whatever their name or whatever they wish to be called."

"And this is where they sit?"

"If they wish."

"Do they find it comfortable?"

"Some do."

"Comfortable enough to give up their deepest, darkest secrets?"

"Therapy isn't about deep, dark secrets. It's about understanding."

"Understanding? You mean why someone flips a light switch on and off repeatedly, or washes their hands for hours."

"Well, I look for the root causes of such things, attempt to bring the individual to understand why these things are learned and try and help them unlearn them. But you're speaking of OCD's, and that's not why you're here."

"No."

"Would you like to sit? Please, we can talk about anything you like."

She shifted her weight onto her heels and spun away from the chair towards the window. He became aware that she was watching his reflection in the glass. This made him uncomfortable. He shifted nervously in his seat, uncrossed, then re-crossed his legs and let out an audible sigh.

"I'm only here to help you, Detective."

"If that's so, then you're the wrong kind of doctor and you're a few days too late."

"I'm sorry about your loss."

"Of course you are. That's what you're supposed to say, isn't it? Get on my good side, pretend you're my friend, gain my trust."

"Actually, no. I'm not a friend, I'm a professional, and while I'm here to help, there are boundaries. So, in a sense, I'm better than a friend."

"Ok, 'friend,' is there something I want to talk about?"

"Deborah, I really…"

"Detective."

"Of course, please, if…"

"Why is it that you have a hard time with that, hmm? If I were a doctor, would I be addressed as Doctor or as Deborah?"

"If your name was Dr. Thomas Jones, for example, I'd call you Thomas or Tom, depending on your preference. And if you were royalty, I'd still call you Deborah."

"Try and get me at ease, get me to open up…."

"This isn't a game…"

"Presume to know me…."

He nodded to himself and began to write in his legal pad. He wrote for a moment, looked up to find her still staring at him. He then stopped, screwed the cap back on his fountain pen and tossed it, along with the pad, gently onto the coffee table in front of him. He then removed his glasses, folded them and placed them onto the pad.

"Let me tell you what I do know, and this is not being presumptuous. You entered the academy at twenty-two after nearly acing the entrance exam. You graduated top of your class, despite the fact that you had a newborn to take care of. Father of your child non-existent, so it was up to you to raise her, and raise her you did. As an officer, you received numerous decorations and one commendation. You sat for the Detective's exam when you were first eligible and nearly aced that one as well. Your cases have a staggering closure rate. You have never been written up, disciplined or held on administrative leave."

"You've memorized my file quite well."

"You then strike a fellow officer causing him the displacement of several teeth."

"He was out of line."

"According to your CO, that is correct, however it was deemed necessary to provide this "optional" series of discussions with me to sort things out."

"Optional, huh?" she snorted.

"Your department is afraid that due to the very recent loss of your daughter, you may react in ways detrimental to a peace officer."

"They're afraid of a lawsuit."

"That's one way to look at it, but they also care about your well being. Your record is impeccable. They feel that maybe if you open up and talk about it, given time, this wound can begin to heal."

"It will never heal. She was my world."

"Tell me about her."

"No. Show's over."

She was staring straight up now, straight up at the ceiling tiles with such detachment as someone looking at clouds. He realized that he was not going to make inroads with her, that his summary of today's session to her CO would be not of non-cooperation, which it was, but of a person who needs time to heal. He felt for her, as her situation was difficult. He would later find himself recommending her for active duty, since that would at least keep her mind focused on something familiar.

"Is there anything at all you wish to talk about?"

She sat there, ignoring his question, ignoring him, lost to some distant thought that no one, save herself, would ever know about.

"Time's up," he said.

Chapter 5

Detective Eisen slid on her sunglasses despite the clouds that threatened rain overhead. She spotted the unmarked car parked at the curb and climbed in, slamming the car door shut behind her.

"Smug asshole."

"It went well then," her partner, Detective Mark Erikson added dryly.

"What the fuck do they want? Seriously!"

"The captain just wants to make sure you're ok."

"I'm fine."

Erikson gave her a look of mock agreement.

"Fuck off."

"Com'on Deb."

"I'm fine, OK? Why is that so difficult to believe?"

"You punched Durkowski."

"He deserved it."

"No doubt, but just the same, you know the road."

"One way street..."

"Deb."

"Alright, alright."

"Just play ball with them."

"What's the point?"

"Deb, if that shrink sends back a report of you being difficult with him, the captain will put you behind a desk."

"I'll quit."

"And do what? Mall security? Private sector? Not likely. You're a cop and you need to stay a cop."

"Let's drop it."

"Deb, I'm serious. The department is worried, I'm worried. For Christ's sake, look at it from their perspective. You've experienced a great loss, you're angry and you're carrying a loaded weapon."

"Is that what you think? Hmm? That's I'm a risk to others?"

"No, that's not what I'm saying."

"That I'm dangerous?"

"Deb, com'on..."

"No, you com'on. I want to know what you think!"

"I think," he said then paused, catching his nerve, "that maybe you just need time off. Take some time to grieve."

"Do you have a smoke," she asked, barely allowing him to finish his sentence as she pushed in the button of the cigarette lighter.

"You don't smoke."

"I didn't ask you if I smoked."

He handed her his pack of cigarettes. She shook a cigarette out of the pack and lit it from the car lighter.

"Deb, I really wish," Erikson began, catching her stare.

"You're one to talk," she said flatly.

"At least crack the window."

What did he wish? He thought to himself. How can he answer that? He looked over at her. She seemed content now, smoking her cigarette and lost in thought. He knew her thoughts were on her child, how could they not be? He wanted so badly to be able to reach out to her, to be a source of comfort, someone from whom she could find solace. He was her partner, after all. Why couldn't she think of him in her time of need?

Then he felt selfish. This is her time, her moment of need, why did he want her to think of him? He knew that one. That was easy. He wanted her to think of him, even if only a fraction of how he thought of her.

He knew he loved her, knew it not long after they were partners. There was something about her he was drawn to. At first he couldn't place it. Sure, she was attractive, but not in a conventional way. Her face was angular, masculine even, given the bone structure and high cheekbones. She looked great however she wore her hair and despite not wearing much make-up, she always looked radiant. But what some men would find unattractive, Erikson found irresistible in his partner.

But that was just it; they were partners. And he sensed that she didn't feel the same way. The last thing he wanted was for there to be any uneasiness between them. In this relationship, where he counted on her and she counted on him, any variable that intruded could prove fatal. They watched each other's backs and knew that if east ever went west, they'd risk their lives for each other.

That was what he told himself when he wondered why he could never summon the courage to say anything.

31

Yet there was something deeper, something that kept him from ever saying anything; something Erikson couldn't even admit to himself.

He watched her smoke the last of her cigarette before turning his attention back to road. They traveled for quite some time in silence. This was nothing unusual. He knew his attempts to gain her attention by glancing at her from time to time would be ignored. He fiddled with the radio, putting on that god awful country station that they both hated, but he couldn't stand it and switched it off. He gave in, as usual, her resolve unbreakable and unyielding.

"I have a surprise for you," he offered.

When that garnered no response, he tapped at the steering wheel for a bit and whistled obnoxiously.

"What?" she demanded.

"Do you remember that case we had a few months back, armed robbery, west end of town, patrol responded to a B&E, security alarm was triggered.

"As I recall, that wasn't a case."

"Yeah, but you do remember that we were sent out the next day to see if things were ok, since, of course, that's a very high tax bracket part of town."

"What of it?"

"The lady who answered the door, what was her name?"

"Don't know."

"Yeah, but we go in and she had this anemic looking little boy, maybe three, and he was bouncing off the walls."

"I remember."

"Do you recall that every picture of that kid that was in the house, on the walls, on the desks, every portrait of was of him in a wheelchair?"

"Maybe."

"You don't remember that?"

"Really, Mark, what's your point? I'm trying really hard not to think of other people's kids right now."

"Sorry. I wasn't thinking…"

"No, it's alright," she said sitting up and turning towards him, "ok, what about it?"

"Do you remember how afraid she was, how she kept asking us to leave?"

"Yeah."

"We have a new case that is eerily similar."

"How so?"

"Same zip code, wealthy couple, robbery, but this time, with a twist," he said as he arched his eyebrows for effect.

"Are you going to tell me or what?"

"This time, there's a body."

He was hoping to get more of a reaction out of her with this, but she merely returned to staring out the side window.

"You wanna get a drink," he asked next after a few minutes.

He drummed on the steering wheel with his fingers, nodding off the silence with his head.

"Dinner?"

Again, his suggestions were met with silence. It wasn't as if she was ignoring him, but rather, he wasn't there, where ever in her mind 'there' was.

"Fine, you win. We'll go dancing," he said at last, voicing a hidden desire in a half-joking tone. "Salsa, you like to salsa? I know a great place. Maybe Tango. It takes two, ya know?"

She turned towards him with a pained expression and tried to offer a smile. Her eyes moist, not yet on the verge of tears, but there was emotion there.

"Just drop me off at home, Mark, I just want to go to sleep."

Chapter 6

Judas couldn't make out the figure passing through his doorway, but he felt no fear. The movements of this man were familiar, but he could not place him. The robes that covered him were drawn tight and cut long, longer than this man's frame could accommodate, causing his feet to be covered. Judas could not tell if this man was barefoot or not.

Judas rose from the table at which he sat. He crossed over to the man and placed both hands upon the man's shoulders.

"I have nothing to offer. I wish I had some wine, some fruit, but I have none at the moment. But if you need a place to rest, I can offer you shelter."

"You have a great deal more to offer than you realize," the man said.

Judas stepped back, removing his hands from the man.

"And what is it that I have to offer?"

"I have watched you Judas, Tax Farmer for the Republic, and have noticed that you are a fair and just man."

"How do you know me?"

"It is a rare occasion when one meets an honest and caring tax collector."

"I say again, how do you know me?"

The man walked past Judas and pulled out a seat at the table. He motioned for Judas to join him and the two men sat down together.

"I have watched you look after my people. I have seen you forgive accounts that could not be met. I have watched you looking after those that, at best, have difficulties looking after themselves."

"Your people?"

The man nodded.

"Who sent you?" Judas asked suspiciously.

"A man."

"'A man' does not spend his time watching tax farmers."

"I watch many things."

"Who sent you? Are you from Rome? Are my collections not enough? Do I not make tribute to the Emperor in a timely and humble fashion?

"I know not of these things."

"You seem to know enough."

"Forgive me, please, I do not wish to offend."

"You do not offend, you arouse suspicion."

"And you will forgive it. You are a good man."

"How do you know the measure of a good man?"

"Come," said the stranger, leaning across the table and grasping the earthen jar, "let us drink to fellowship."

"That jar has no wine."

"Does it not?"

The stranger tilted the jar, causing red wine to flow forth. He poured the wine into two cups and offered one to Judas.

"But I had no wine!"

"Yes, you gave your wine to a poor fellow, his family had none. In fact, you gave them fruit and bread. You gave them hope, you gave them love."

"But how, how can this be?" Judas stammered as he pulled the jar from the stranger's hands, causing the wine to spill freely.

"What you have given freely to others, is given back to you in return."

"Who are you?" Judas demanded, leaping to his feet.

The stranger stood before him and removed his hood. The last thing Judas remembered was a bright light, warm and inviting, filling the room, and leaving him blind.

***

Judas awoke late in the day. His head was pounding and a searing pain ripped across his head every time he tried to open his eyes.

"Mac," he called. "Mac!"

"Yes, I'm here."

"Are the drapes closed?"

"Yes, they are."

"It's so bright."

"Let me," Mac began, "let me get the bandages."

Mac produced and carefully unfolded a beautiful black scarf, plain at first glance, but of exquisite cloth and craftsmanship. He gently shook out its length, letting it fall to the bare, wooden floor. He then held the end gently

37

against Judas' temple and began to wind the length of it lovingly around his head, making sure his eyes were fully covered and tied it off at the base of his head.

"Is that better?"

"Yes, yes" Judas stammered, "yes, thank you, much better."

Mac moved to a side table and poured a glass of water and mixed into it a yellow powder that turned the liquid bright red. He stirred it quietly and handed it to Judas.

"Drink this, it will refresh you."

Judas took the glass and began to drink it slowly. Then he tipped it back and finished it in one gulp. He held the glass out to Mac.

"Will there be anything else?"

"No, Mac."

Mac took the glass and turned to go, but Judas reached out and without knowing exactly where Mac was, grabbed his arm as if by instinct.

"Mac, what day is today?"

"It's two days hence, sir."

"I'm sleeping more, then."

Mac paused to look at his master, the mess of dark hair protruding from the mask wrapped around his eyes, obscuring his face but showing enough of his taut skin. His body was gaunt; always thin but more so this morning, almost painfully so.

"I'm afraid so, sir."

Judas nodded his head as if in agreement to something unspoken. He rubbed at his temples with his palms, trying vainly, as he knew it always was, to ease the pressure.

"He's here, Mac."

"How can you be sure?"

"I'm beginning to have dreams again."

Chapter 7

After dropping Eisen off at her place, Erikson drove around for awhile. He didn't think of where he was going; he just drove aimlessly, street signs becoming meaningless.

He drove into the parking lot of a coffee shop, thinking he might enjoy a cup. He parked, yet couldn't find enough motivation to get out of the car. He sat there the better of fifteen minutes, distracted by the ineffectualness he displayed with his partner. It wasn't just a mere selfish desire to spend time with her. He was genuinely concerned. He wanted to be the one she would rely on, but that was a decision he couldn't make for her.

He continued driving, wandering aimlessly as the sun set and the street lights flickered on. He found himself stopped at a stoplight with a bar on the corner. Without much deliberation as to whether he wanted a drink, he soon found himself inside, eyes adjusting to the darkness.

The bar was a seedy, smoke tainted place. There were two old men at the bar, seated several stools apart. He was ignored by the men as he walked by, and he was hardly noticed by the bartender who only lifted his head and arched his brow rather than ask him what he wanted.

"Beer, whatever's cold on draft."

The bartender pulled the tap and soon Erikson was staring at a tall glass of liquid gold. He took one long sip and closed his eyes as he swallowed.

A loud bang roused Erikson from his bliss. He turned and noticed a man standing uneasily in the doorway. He watched as the man began to walk in a drunken manner towards him. The man brushed past Erikson as if he wasn't there and fell heavily against the bar; one hand digging into his pockets, one hand steadying himself. He produced a fist full of coins and dropped them on the bar. The bartender, without any sign of hesitation that may impart a refusal of service, counted out several coins, then produced a bottle of beer. The man raised the bottle to his lips and drank, not stopping until he slammed the empty bottle on the bar. The drink seemed to steady the man, and when he regained his balance, he sat easily on the stool next to Erikson.

Erikson took note as the bartender walked over, counted out several more coins and produced another beer. The man then pulled long and hard to empty this beer in one try, then slammed the bottle down on the counter. He scooped the remaining coins into his pocket, let out a long burp and walked with a perceivable swagger out the door.

Erikson turned his attention back to his drink but found it was empty. He motioned to the bartender who produced a replacement.

"That guy can knock 'em back, huh?"

The bartender nodded in agreement, but didn't say anything. Erikson found himself nodding too, to ward off the awkwardness of the exchange.

"That guy come in here a lot?"

The bartender shrugged his shoulders.

"Not a lot of regulars around here, huh?"

The bartender lifted his arms to say he didn't think so.

Erikson finished his second drink and pushed himself back from the bar. Still seated, he caught the bartenders lifted eyebrows, asking if he'd care for another. Erikson shook his head, finally becoming proficient at this game.

As Erikson entered the car, something caught his eye. He paused, his spine resting at the edge of the seatback. He got out and walked around the car. Somebody had stolen the hub covers off the wheels. He shook his head, not in disbelief because in this part of town, if it's not nailed down, its free game, but that he parked the car in direct eyesight. He could see midway up the wheels through the dingy windows of the bar. The man who drank the beers had so distracted him that someone could have stolen the car and he wouldn't have noticed. What's more, he began to realize, is that taking note of this man had pushed his mind away from the reason he was here. The drinks he had gone to consume to steady his will had done nothing. He got back into the car as if possessed by something that he knew was a foregone conclusion.

He drove around for awhile before spotting a young woman walking along the sidewalk. She walked very slowly, stopping every so often to wave at passing motorists. He pulled up alongside, lowered the passenger window and tapped the horn.

"Hey handsome," the young woman said as she strutted up to the car.

"What are you doing?" Erikson asked.

"Walkin'. What about you?"

"Just driving."

"Want some company?"

"How old are you?"

"As old as you want me to be."

She crossed her arms and leaned into the car, giving Erikson a sample of her small cleavage, hidden behind a thin gauze dress shirt tied up high and tight across her sternum.

"You a cop?" she asked, smacking her gum through an open mouth to accentuate each word.

"I might be."

"Yeah, you're a cop. I can tell."

"How?"

"Well, the car, you know, fucking boring."

"Get in."

She opened the door and got in right leg first, forcing her to pull her left leg under, slowly and intentionally flashing Erikson her sheer panties in the process. She sat forward, legs open slightly, making it easier for him to slide his hand up her very short skirt if he so desired.

"You're a cop, I know it."

"How so?"

"I've seen you before."

"Oh yeah?"

"Yeah. Aaronson or something."

"Wow, you're good," he offered, wanting to end her inquiry.

"You got a partner, don't you?"

"We all have partners."

"Yours, it's a chick right?"

Erikson pulled the car over near the mouth of an alley. He wanted to get rid of her now, go back to before he pulled over to talk to her, before she could identify him. As he was bringing the car to a stop, something came over him that he found strangely liberating. Rather than stop and ask her to get out of the car, he accelerated, turning the car sharply and drove into the alley. He continued slowly down the deserted lane until he found a vacant stall under the overhang of a building's loading dock and parked. The area was littered with trash and debris and Erikson thought from its state of disuse, nobody would bother them.

He pulled out a napkin and asked the girl for her gum. She grinned, turned her head and spit it out the open window. She then turned to face Erikson, arranging her legs in a cross legged fashion, purposefully showing off her wares.

Erikson reached out and untied the knot that kept her shirt together. He pulled at the fabric as it fell away from her small, pert breasts. He cupped his hand around her left breast, feeling his way around it gently, as if this were the most beautiful and precious breast in the world. He worked his hand slowly until he held the soft nub of a nipple between his thumb and forefinger. He pressed on it until it grew and became hard, echoing the same change in physicality he now felt.

"Mmmm, oh that feels good," she said.

"Don't say anything."

"Oh baby, I won't say anything to anybody," she began, a bit too loudly for the moment.

"No, I meant be quiet."

"Oh," she responded, looking down and reaching a hand out towards Erikson's crotch. When she made contact with the bulge in the fabric, he swatted her hand away.

"Don't," he warned.

43

He closed his eyes and slid his hand slowly down her side, along her ribcage, feeling each rib in pronounced detail. He kept going, finding the top of her hip, and then sliding gently along its path until it led him to an impasse at the top of her skirt. Without asking, she undid her skirt and pulled it off, allowing Erikson free passage further south.

He found the hip bone again, tracing his finger down, over the thin, sheer fabric. He moved very slowly now, taking what seemed an eternity to them both to finally come to rest on her clitoris. She inhaled sharply now, but it wasn't the girl that he heard, it was Eisen. With eyes closed, he was with her now, gently making motions with his fingers around her womanhood, feeling the moisture through the almost non-existent fabric.

He stopped only to seize Eisen by the hips and pull her forcefully towards him. This caused the girl to hit her head on the door handle.

"Ow!"

"Sorry."

"I don't do rough!"

"Sorry," he said, eyes open again, "now please, be quiet."

He closed his eyes again as he hooked his fingers on her panties and pulled them from her hips, down her thighs, past her knees and finally off. He spread her thighs apart and paused only to free himself from the fabric that confined him. Eyes still closed, in his mind's eye, he saw Eisen before him, lying naked, waiting for him, wanting him.

He entered her and felt such a rush of exhilaration. He could see Eisen's face as she closed her eyes and sharply turned her head upwards, clearly enjoying how he felt inside her.

"Oh baby, yeah, fuck me, baby, fuck me," the girl moaned.

Erikson opened his eyes to see the girl, head turned sideways, staring without emotion at the seat back, muttering her remarks without a hint of emotion on her face.

"Shut the fuck up," Erikson shouted.

A look of fear rose up in the girl as her eyes became wide. She turned away from Erikson, away from his crazed look and focused her gaze on the glove box.

Erikson shut his eyes again, working his hips back and forth. He could see her again, he could feel her around him, pulling him, squeezing. He could feel her hands on his shoulders now, could see directly into her as she held his gaze. Her breathing became sharper, faster, until she squeezed his shoulders, arched her back and let out a long wail. She squeezed him rapidly now, losing all control in this moment. Erikson couldn't hold back and came along with her, letting out an almost primal scream.

When he stopped, he opened his eyes. The girl was staring up at the roof of the car, paying no attention to him. Her hands were on his shoulders and while he felt her around him, he knew that she did not come.

He pulled himself away from her, watched her as she reached for the paper napkin she refused for her gum and cleaned herself. As he tucked himself back into his trousers, she pulled up her panties and fastened her skirt around her waist. He felt a wave of nausea come over him, not of being physically ill, but of guilt. He felt unclean. Not because she was a prostitute, but because his basest desire led him to settle for something much less than what he so desperately wanted.

He watched her now, only her, as she pulled the ends of her shirt together, tying the knot just below her breasts.

Erikson pulled out a cigarette and lit it. The girl stared straight ahead now, through the windshield and

45

focused on the brick wall in front of the car. He took a few more drags and saw that the woman did not move.

"Are you going to arrest me now?"

"Why would I do that?"

"You get a free fuck and then you arrest me. I know the routine."

"I wouldn't do that."

"All you pigs do that."

"I'm not a pig," he offered.

Erikson backed the car out and drove up the alley toward the street. She pulled at the handle and tried to get out, but Erikson grabbed her arm and pulled her back.

"Com'on man, really? I've got a kid. I can't afford to be off the street. I can't fucking believe you're going to arrest me after this."

Erikson moved his hand towards his belt, past his handcuffs and dug into his pockets. He produced several large bills and stuck them into her hand. She looked at him with wide eyes, certain it was a trick.

"Get out."

She got out of the car and began walking the opposite way down the sidewalk. As Erikson drove off, he noticed that not once did she look back.

Chapter 8

"This is the one," began Donovan, "this one is quite amazing!"

He cradled the revolver lovingly in his right hand. He held it forward, sighting it, resisting the weight of the heavy barrel that caused it to droop downward.

"Yep, this here is a Smith and Wesson, .44 magnum. My uncle has one," he said grinning at Slava. He then turned toward Slava and mindlessly pointed the gun on him.

Slava effortlessly snatched the gun away from him and shook it in Donovan's face.

"Nyet, nyet, nyet! First, never point at what you won't shoot! And this, this piece of shit!"

He slammed the gun on the table and picked up a black semi-automatic.

"Now this," Slava countered, "this is colt 1911. Only gun you ever need. Seven shot, .45 caliber. It knock men down. No big upward recoil and boom, boom of magnum. Recoil straight back. Nice, accurate, and indestructible!"

"What about this one," Donovan countered, picking up a smaller, similar looking gun.

"9mm? Piece of shit."

"Oh, come on!"

"Look," he said, running a finger along the bottom side of the gun, "this plastic."

"Composite."

"Shit!"

"It holds 16 rounds compared to your seven."

"Sixteen rounds," Slava moaned sarcastically, "who needs sixteen rounds? How many times you missing target?"

Slava snatched this weapon away from Donovan and gave him a not so subtle push away from the table.

"Go, little baby, go do baby things. Leave man's work to me!"

Donovan sulked away and saw that Mac was smiling and shaking his head.

"What's so funny?"

Mac said nothing, kept polishing his boots, working them to a mirror's shine.

"You guys are no help. Nobody speaks, nobody says anything. This isn't what I..."

"Had in mind?" asked Mac, finishing Donovan's thoughts.

"Yeah."

"Afraid we're not doing God's work?"

"Well, kind of."

"Who said anything about doing God's work?"

48

Donovan sat heavily in the club chair across from Mac. He slid his feet forward and exhaled loudly. He then noticed Mac's attention focused on his scuffed shoes. He slid his feet back in embarrassment.

"You know, I can fix those," Mac said, nodding to his shoes.

"No, I'm good. Thanks."

Mac went back to polishing his boots. He finished the right boot and compared it to the left boot.

"Almost there," he grinned.

Donovan sat watching him scrub the other boot, then add a thick layer of wax and work it around with a sock. Mac felt his eyes on him, but ignored his audience and began to hum softly to himself.

"You're his caretaker, right?"

"Yep," Mac replied, not looking up, not ceasing from the task at hand.

"And Crispis, he's the driver."

"You catch on quick."

"So what does the Russian guy do?"

Mac stopped polishing and looked up at Donovan.

"Who's that?"

"Who's that?!?! Him over there," he pointed. "That tall muscular guy. Mr. Brooding.

"Slava?"

"Yes, Slava!"

Mac shrugged his shoulder, "Slava does what needs to be done, I guess. Things that not many people want to do."

"And what is that?"

"Whatever it is that needs doing," Mac replied, looking down again as his hands worked their way around the boot.

Mac started to smile, nodding his head as he worked the polish into the old leather. When he was satisfied, he reached for a brush and began working his boots. He looked up to see the young priest looking despondent.

"Listen," Mac began, edging his chair forward, closer to Donovan, "don't expect Slava to tell you his life's story. In fact, don't expect him to say too much. Three things you need to know about him. First, his English has never been very good. Second, his story is not something he'd ever tell you."

Donovan rocked forward, eager to listen.

"And third, you don't want to know his story. You won't like it. He wasn't no victim."

Donovan sat back, feeling defeated. He starred at the man across from him, once again his full attention on shining his boots.

"Why me, then?"

"We been wonderin' the same thing," Mac laughed.

He then put his boot down, next to the other and beamed with pride.

"There! Good as new. You know," he leaned in again to Donovan, "I bought those boots in 1932. Bought 'em brand new and they still look as good as when I first put them on. See what a little polish will do! You sure you won't try a little? You'll be glad you did!"

Donovan sat up and picked up a can of polish off the floor. He slid off his shoes and began working them as Mac did.

"There you go, get it in there."

Donovan kept on it, rubbing in the wax, around and around the shoe.

"You know, we're just as curious as you are."

"About Slava?"

"No, not Slava, about you."

50

"What's to wonder?"

"Why he picked you."

"I don't know, you tell me."

"You see, I been here a while. I've taken care of him. I know the history of the people he's had before us, long before us. It's an oral tradition, nothing written down, that's his way. So I know who was here before and why, and more importantly how. But you, you don't fit in with all those that have gone before you."

"Yeah, well what's different about me?"

"For starters, you're a priest."

"He doesn't like holy men, huh?"

"No, no, we've had true believers; zealots and such. Just never before have we had someone so," he hesitated as he searched for the words.

"So what?"

"So, not quite dead."

"What?"

"He saves, that's what he does. He's a healer. You saw that last night, with that boy."

Mac eased back in his seat and looked back at Slava and watched him a moment as he cleaned the guns. Slava did not look up, but nodded as Mac had expected.

"What I want to know is how you got here. You weren't dying. You weren't a soul in need of saving."

"A soul in need of saving is a matter of opinion," Donovan replied.

He sank deeper into the chair, felt himself getting lost in the depths of the fabric. He felt safe, felt this way for the first time outside the confines of the church. He felt as if maybe Mac already knew his story. His eyes weren't piercing, nor prying; they just held the sympathetic look of a man who's lived a difficult life and emerged from those lessons with a keen understanding of how things might work. This was what Donovan was after, he thought.

"Is there, uh, any way to get a cigarette?"

Without warning, a half empty pack of cigarettes hit him in the chest and fell into his lap. He looked up, past Mac, whose gazed remained frozen and saw Slava nod once, and then return his attention to the guns.

"Ok," he said, then inhaled, gesturing a thank you for the light that Mac offered, "great, you were expecting that. This won't be entertaining, I'm sure. I haven't fallen from grace or anything like that. But," he paused and drew on the smoke again, "I'm quick out of the gate and I've got a good start."

I decided to become a man of the Lord early. I mean really, early. Most men find His love and decide to follow it in their teens, maybe in their twenties. Not me, I was hooked at eight years old.

I was kicked out of kindergarten, of all things. Hyperactive is what they called it. Trouble maker, attention deficit, whatever; they just couldn't get my attention.

My parents took me out of the neighborhood school and sent me across town to this small Catholic school. They had no buses, my father having to drive me early before work. He was a garbage man, so getting up early was no problem for him, but back then they had no before school care. The church at the school had a 6am service, so that's where he dropped me. I was to wait in the church until the school opened at 7:30.

It was a beautiful old building, stained glass, old statues, tall ceilings; it was everything a church should be. At first I'd just sit in the back pew and not even listen, not pay attention to what was being spoken, but to what the building was telling me. The Stations of the Cross I didn't understand at first, so I made up stories that helped it make sense.

After a few weeks, one of the older parishioners returned from the hospital and began playing the organ again. What was his name? Mickey, I think, yeah. Mr. Mickey, he was old, a retired school teacher, and every morning he'd walk up to me, put his hand on my shoulder, and smile at me. He'd then begin his climb up the narrow, unforgiving staircase to the organists' nest.

His music changed things for me. For the first time, I felt something; I felt the church really come alive. It was the music that was missing. It became pageantry. I listened now, raptly at what the priest had to say, how the handful of people attending the mass, all of them elderly, transcended their feeble bodies every time they rejoiced his name and cried out "Amen!" As a whole, they became stronger and I thought, at first, it was the priest's doing. I thought he was all powerful. How could I not, he was a tall, handsome man, with thick black framed glasses. His face held a kindly expression. Everyone loved him.

I looked forward to going every morning. Often times I'd be the one rousing my father from his sleep, making sure he was up and could shower and shave and drop me off so I wouldn't miss a minute of the service.

It was like this until second grade, when I turned eight, that they added a lunchtime service. This corresponded with my lunch recess at school, so every day I ate hurriedly, skipped recess and went to mass. Everyday! A child skipping recess! But I was thirsty, filling myself up with God's word, with his love, with all the things I wasn't getting at home.

I never ate breakfast, mainly because my father didn't. And with not eating much lunch, I was weak. One day at lunch time mass I fainted. Nobody would have noticed had I not hit my head on the pew in front of me, causing a loud "clunk" right as the priest asked for a moment of quiet prayer.

When I awoke, light was streaming through the stained glass windows, silhouetting His image. Ok, maybe it wasn't Him, but to an eight year old, it was. And that was it. I was hooked.

I dedicated my life to his words. I learned the Bible, inside and out, chapter and verse. There was a time when I could quote it for you, in Latin. I was being touted as a young genius of theology. While my classmates were playing football and learning about girls, I was finding my spirituality and studying God.

I was prepared to enter seminary when I was given the opportunity of a lifetime. I was summoned to Rome to study at the Vatican. I was what, eighteen, going off to Europe by myself. I'd never before been outside the city. My parents never vacationed. To my knowledge, the only time they've ever been away from home was on their honeymoon, and that was a meager getaway.

Donovan sat silent, looking at Mac's brilliant boots. He nodded a few times, and then looked past Mac at Slava, who paid him no mind.

"How old are you?"

"Pardon?"

"I guess I should have said, 'how old are you, kid?' since you ain't much older than twenty-five, am I right?

"I'm twenty-four, yeah, good guess."

"Why ain't you in Rome?"

"People," Donovan answered quickly. "It was a choice between dusty books or reaching out to the people. As much as I loved my time in Rome, which was brief, I knew my calling was as a conduit of God for the people. To reach out and help someone find their true path to God, or to assist them to regain their footing, that's what I desired."

Donovan once again focused his attention on the ground. He nodded his head again.

"I had it all; every young priest's dream. They gave me a congregation. I wasn't in the least bit politically motivated, but they hinted at great things for me, things for which I doubted any man of God should have an appetite."

"But all men have appetites," Mac interrupted.

At this, Donovan fell silent. He looked Mac in the eyes. Mac's eyes held sympathy. He simply shrugged at the young priest and bent to pick up his boots. After a moment he rose and walked out of the room.

Donovan began to weep silently. He thought about appetites, about wanting. All he had ever wanted was to serve God. He knew nothing of wanting anything else, never allowed himself the curiosity that distraction could bring. He knew of sin, understood he was born of original sin, but deep inside, he always believed that sin was for other men. Other men fell into temptation. Other men resisted God's teachings and fell headlong unto their dark desires. Not Donovan, though. He had remained pure in thought and spirit.

Until that one Sunday, exactly one year before Judas made himself known to him. That was a special mass. Donovan was celebrating two years at his Parrish. He put together what he thought was a celebration of God's love and forgiveness. He planned to speak of God's plan for us all, his wisdom, his forgiveness, his absolute love for all his children.

He had finished the opening prayer and had walked before the altar to address the parishioners, something he preferred to do rather than preaching from the elevated pulpit.

He looked around, as was his custom, and then he froze. There, maybe twelve pews back, was a woman who he had never seen before. She sat with rapt attention. He found it hard to meet her gaze, so he looked around again, cleared his throat and was about to begin his sermon when he looked at her again. No words could escape, everything held as if in a vacuum. He suddenly realized that she was the most beautiful thing he had ever laid eyes on. He had never looked upon such beauty, but there it was, in guise of a woman, a creature of the Lord, before him, humble and waiting on his words. But words failed him; he forgot his sermon, his carefully rehearsed speech. He felt shame, felt something insidious inside him. He knew right away what this was. He felt desire.

Slava finished with his task and was watching Donovan quietly from across the room. He couldn't know what was causing the young priest tears, and he couldn't bring forth any emotional connection to make himself care. He viewed the young priest as an oddity. He couldn't guess what Judas wanted with this man, and it was beyond his desire to find out.

Without taking his eyes off Donovan, Slava slid a clip into his .45 and worked a round in the chamber. He then holstered it and picked up a 9mm he had been working on. He walked around the table and stood in front of Donovan. So lost in remembrance was the young priest that he didn't notice Slava at first. Slava thrust the grip of the 9mm in front of his face, wrenching him from his thoughts.

"You take, is good gun. Not good as .45, but it do for you."

Donovan reached up and took the gun, not saying a word.

"You get holster. Mac give you," Slava commanded, looking sideways at him now. "You get up, come, we have work to do."

Chapter 9

Detective Erikson pulled the tape away from the door jamb and pushed the heavy door open. It swung easily on its hinges, almost as if it weighed nothing at all.

The two detectives entered and found themselves in a grand hall, stretching forward at least one hundred feet to the other end.

Erikson whistled aloud.

"Yeah," Eisen replied, "pretty tacky, huh?"

"On the contrary, this is amazing. Look at how big it is. Can you imagine all the parties you can have here? You can easily fit at least three hundred people in here."

"The bigger the room, the more you have to clean."

"Oh, I think if you can afford this place, you can afford to pay someone else to clean it."

"Where's the action?"

"Oh, no action."

"I thought you said it was a murder."

"I said there was a body."

"Which is it?"

"Come," he said, motioning her to follow.

They walked across the great hall to an alcove to the far right. Here, they found a pair of large doors propped open. Eisen peered in and saw that it was a library, maybe a quarter of the great hall and two stories, floor to ceiling lined with books.

Erikson motioned for her to follow him to the fireplace. There, perpendicular to the massive stone hearth was a chair, modern in construction, opposite a massive white leather sofa. Between them was a glass coffee table.

"Ok, where is it?"

"There," Erickson answered, pointing to the floor in front of the sofa.

"Where's the blood? Where's the tape outline?"

"Oh, he didn't die here, not in any manner that makes sense."

"Oh, for fuck's sake, Mark."

"Ok, here's what happens. This is according to what we could figure out from the mother. She's in observation."

"Did she do it?"

"No. She's just off the deep end. I guess watching your husband kill your child will do that to you."

"So the husband did it?"

"No, but she thinks he did."

Eisen shook her head and gave her partner a cold look.

"Sorry," Erikson said, realizing she was in no better mood today. "Here's what we got. Group of men break in, no alarm sounds, they hold them hostage, threaten to harm their crippled son unless they're given the contents of the safe and then make a deal with the family to that effect."

"What kind of deal."

"Not sure exactly, but according to the wife, they heal the kid in exchange for the combination to the safe."

"What?"

"Yeah, crazy huh?"

"They healed him?" Eisen asked.

"From what the wife says, this one guy takes him from the wheel chair, disconnects all the gizmos that are keeping him alive and cradles the kid into his chest. He then goes into some kind of trance, convulses or something and they both crash to the floor. Then, and this is where I'm thinking maybe the wife is nuts, the kid gets up, calls his mother's name and hurries over to her. Something she's never seen nor heard."

"So what about…"

"Oh, it gets better! The group of men carries this one guy out, he's comatose or something. The husband, doesn't now what to do. This guy is old enough to be this woman's father. You know, old guy gets money, marries some trophy, promises wealth in exchange for looking like the big swinging dick at the country club."

"I get it."

"So any way, what do you think he does?"

"Spare me the mystery."

"He comes to his senses. Now this is from his statement. He calls the police. As soon as he hangs up the phone, the kid begins to convulse. The mother is screaming, call an ambulance and what not. The kid drops to the floor; he's not breathing. The paramedics, when they get there, and they got there quick, 'cause that's what money can do, grab the kid and off they go to the hospital. We even got a statement from the paramedics that the wife was screaming bloody murder at her husband that he killed the kid, something about a promise he broke. Medics never revive the kid, he's listed as DOA."

"A promise?"

"Yeah, apparently this promise had a catch."

"A catch?"

"That they tell no one of what took place. I guess that included not calling the cops."

"And what does the husband say?"

"Don't know. We couldn't get anything out of him before his lawyer showed up. Then he was out the door."

"You couldn't hold him?"

"On what grounds? He made a phone call and that act of dialing a phone was what killed his kid? The wife is probably out of her mind. This perp more than likely pulled some kind of ruse that gave them time enough to get away before the old man came to his senses and called it in."

"But you said he got up and walked."

"That's what the wife said."

"And you don't believe that?"

Erikson looked at his partner for a moment. He understood her loss and realized that it may have been a mistake to bring her into this. His excitement over getting such a bizarre case quickly turned to pity as he motioned to her with open arms.

"Deb," he offered.

"No," she responded, "I'm fine."

"I'm sorry."

"Shut up," she said as she ignored his pity and looked around the room.

"The safe?" Eisen inquired.

"The technicians got that covered."

"Good. Let's go see the wife. I want to hear this from her."

Chapter 10

"May I have a cigarette?"

Janine Davenport looked nervously around the room. The powder blue walls, originally intended to calm, made her nervous. She sat at the table, her right elbow stretched across the surface, allowing her right hand to reach the back of her neck. She tapped the table top nervously with her left hand, exposing the wrist band with the hospital code that Eisen was only too familiar.

"I'm sorry, I don't think you can smoke here," Detective Eisen said.

"Uh, maybe we could make an exception," Erikson offered, smiling at his partner.

He produced a small box of cigarettes and handed it to Mrs. Davenport. She took the package and looked at it with curiosity, turning it over and over in her hand.

"What kind are these?"

"Uh, they're British."

"And where would one find cigarettes like these?"

"I pick them up at a cigar shop," he answered, producing a lighter.

"They any good?" she winked.

"Only one way to find out," he smiled as she leaned in to accept his light.

"Mrs. Davenport," Detective Eisen began.

"Janine, please," she corrected, starring directly at Erikson now, "call me Janine."

Eisen stifled a snicker, turning it into a cough.

"Janine," she emphasized sarcastically, then caught herself as she realized that she was about to question her about her dead son. She ran a hand through her hair, scratching gently at her scalp, trying to change her impression of this woman.

"I'm terribly sorry for your loss."

Janine's smile, fixed on Erickson, immediately began to crack. She placed her full attention on her cigarette, watching the tiny curls of tobacco burn a bright red.

"That bastard," she muttered.

"Who?"

"Who? Him! He killed my son."

"Janine, please, we need your help," Eisen said. "We'd like to talk about the events of the evening, specifically the men who broke in and held you hostage."

"Events of the evening? Yeah, it was an event alright."

"You've never seen these men before?"

Janine turned to Erikson once again, offering a smile while holding back tears, something she had perfected for the better part of the decade, a part she played to perfection in her loveless marriage.

"That's what I said. They wore ski masks, except for the one, the one in charge, he didn't wear one," she said, pulling a piece of tobacco off her tongue with an elegantly manicured pinky.

"Could you describe him," Eisen prodded.

"No."

Eisen looked up at her partner, sensing that she was getting nowhere.

"Janine," Erikson began, "do you remember what he looked like?"

"These are really good," she said, ignoring his question. "I didn't think I'd ever like an unfiltered cigarette, but these are really tasty."

"Thanks," Erikson replied. "Now, about the man?"

"I don't know. Every time I think of him, try to recall what he looked like, he looks different. I know that sounds weird. He was plain, nondescript, maybe European, maybe not, I don't know." She drew heavily on her cigarette and exhaled. "You know, for what he did, you think I'd remember him exactly, but I don't. Maybe I'm blocking it out, but I don't think I'm blocking out the right parts, you know?"

"You don't seem very angry when you speak of this guy," Eisen added.

"Why would I be angry?"

"For the death of your son."

"What do you know about it?"

"With your help, I'll know more."

"Yeah, well he didn't kill my son, he saved him. That fat bastard of a lousy husband killed him! All his

64

money and what to show for it, a big house, a hot wife and what do I get? A cripple! From birth, and all I hear is that it's all my fault! All my doing, my big tits leaked, maybe. Yeah, well that's what got me here; I paid the price of admission. He didn't mind, as long as he got to show them off to his fat cat friends and business acquaintances. He rarely paid any attention to our son, oh sure he paid the medical bills, donated to charities; put himself out there like some big caring philanthropist. But it was all for show. Everything was for show."

"Janine," Erikson began, prompted by Eisen's stare and sensing her decreasing patience, "according to your husband, this man disconnected the life line to your child."

"He made us promise."

"Promise? Promise what?"

"He could heal him he said. He would heal him, if we promised never to speak of it to anyone."

"Let me get this straight," Eisen said, "these men break into your home, hold you hostage and then make promises to heal your child? Am I getting this right?"

"Yes."

"And they'd get what in return for performing such a miracle?"

"Everything in our safe."

"Which was?"

"Everything."

"Please be more specific."

Janine impatiently blew a lungful of smoke at Detective Eisen and laughed.

"Let's see, several million in cash, maybe a few million in jewelry and several trade secrets I didn't know about nor cared to know."

"Sounds like a deal," joked Erikson.

"Yeah, except that fat fucker went against the deal."

65

"How?"

"He called the cops. As soon as he started dialing, my son started convulsing, spitting up, choking," she trailed off, crying now into her hands.

"How could he possibly heal him?" Eisen whispered to herself out loud.

Eisen tried not to feel pity for this woman, but felt it anyway. Maybe she wasn't the stone cold gold digger she took her for, but she was an opportunist. Still, she found herself moved by how emotional this woman was and wondered if it was because it was too soon and hit too close to home.

She reached a hand out to comfort her, but it stopped shy of the woman's shoulder. She thought maybe she should say something, but instead brought her hand up over her own mouth and walked quickly from the room.

Erikson turned to follow, but stopped, realizing that he still had a job to do.

"What's her problem," Janine asked sarcastically.

"She has a call to make," he said, covering for his partner.

"Well, you're much better company," she said, wiping her eyes. "Are you married?"

"No," Erikson replied, producing another cigarette and lighting it in his lips, "here."

"Mmmm," she exhaled, "have any kids?"

"No."

"Your partner?"

"She had a daughter."

He found Eisen in a small waiting room at the end of the hallway, sitting alone in a chair by the window. She didn't acknowledge his presence as he walked up nor did she make note of him as he sat down beside her.

"I'm sorry, Deb."

"Do you believe her?"

"Listen, if you need to talk about this…"

"Do you believe her?" Eisen interrupted, still not making eye contact.

"She's awfully mad at her husband, doesn't sound mad nor even the slightest bit vengeful towards this man or group of burglars. I don't know Deb. It's kinda hard to believe that someone can just heal a damaged body."

"How'd he do it?"

"Maybe he didn't do it. Maybe he faked it."

"Faked it how?"

"I don't know, drugs maybe. Perhaps he injected something into the IV's as he pulled the wires, something that would shock him into seeming like he was responsive. Maybe," he paused. "Do you believe this could have happened?"

"I don't know," Eisen said, shaking her head.

"Deb, what if she was in on it? What if it was just an act to get the old man to open the safe? Who knows what kind of drug could have been slipped to the boy, make him calm a few minutes before all his organs fail? This sounds like a con. How many cons have we cracked, maybe not as unique as this, nor as heart wrenching, but com'on."

"Yeah, maybe you're right. But she did seem pretty broken up, though."

"Maybe she's one hell of an actress."

"God, I'd hate to think that."

"She lasted, what, ten years in a sham of a marriage? I'd call that pretty damn good acting. Of course, money is a great motivator. Still, nothing is surprising anymore, though, is it?"

"In this line of work, no, unfortunately you think the worst of people.

"There you go," he said.

"But doesn't that anger you?"

"Ah, I've seen too much shit to let it piss me off."

"But when it involves a child?"

Erikson nodded his head in agreement as he watched his partner's attention become lost to the outside world once again.

"Deb," he offered, reaching across the table, but finding nothing but sticky stains embedded in the cracked plastic table top as she evaded his touch.

"Com'on" she said getting up, "we need to talk to the husband."

Chapter 11

"That miserable bitch!"

Mr. Davenport was standing now, both fists clenched and pressed firmly into the massive modern ensemble of materials that comprised his desk. His fists, red now, trembled as he bore his full weight onto them.

"We just need to go over your statement," Erikson calmly interjected.

"She wanted that damn kid! Not me! I had a family already! She knew that, she knew!"

"All you wanted was what, arm candy?"

"And what's wrong with that? I've made something of myself. I've amassed a fortune, so don't I deserve a hot young wife? I kill myself all these years so my first wife can get fat and spend all my money. Then she takes half of everything I've owned, half of everything I provided her with? Maybe you don't realize this Detective Erikson, but a man of my stature deserves, no, he demands something nice on his arm, and in his bed!"

Erikson put up his palms as he turned to face his partner, mouthing an "its all yours" to her.

"Mr. Davenport," Eisen began, "you've said in a statement that what you saw, and in your wife's statement she basically said the same thing, but what puzzles me is what happened after the robbers left. She said you made a phone call."

"I did."

"To whom?"

"What do you mean, 'to whom?' To you people!"

"Why?"

"Are you deaf? Are you stupid?" He looked to Erikson for some allegiance, but found none. He was off his desk now, pacing behind it, mumbling and cursing Eisen now. She smiled inwardly as his girth made each breath come in a painful gasp.

"Your wife," Eisen continued, "said you made an arrangement with these men that you were to tell no one of what happened. Is this true?"

"Tell me Detective, what would you do if someone was holding your child hostage and threatening his life?"

"I'm not arguing with you, I'm just trying to piece this together."

"What would you do?" he demanded.

"I'd comply with their request."

"Damn straight you would!"

Eisen looked at her partner, who looked back at her with raised eyebrows.

"What did you lose?" she asked.

"Money."

"Money? How much?"

"Millions," he said falling heavily into his large leather chair.

"Millions," Eisen repeated, "wow, that's rough."

"Indeed."

"Just Millions? Anything else?"

"Deeds to several properties, insurance policies, things like that."

"Anything else?"

"Nothing I can think of?"

"Any jewelry?"

"Yes, probably her damned jewelry, too!"

"Anything else?"

"Not that I'm at liberty to discuss."

"Trade secrets?"

Davenport slid his massive hands across the desk, brought them together with a clap and brought them under his chin. He starred at Eisen, almost as if he was trying to make her uncomfortable.

Eisen stood her ground, she bobbed her head and raised her eyebrows as if to communicate that an answer was expected. She then smiled at him.

"There may have been some items related to our corporation and in our corporation's best interests and that of our shareholders, I'm not at liberty to discuss them."

"Are you quoting your lawyer?"

"Something like that," he smiled.

"Fair enough," Eisen obliged. "Tell me, are you over extended?"

"That's none of your business."

"I can make it my business."

"Are you accusing me of something Detective Eisen? The last time I checked, I was witness to a murder, the murder of my son."

"According to your wife," Eisen countered, "you thought little of your son."

"How dare you!"

"I can understand," she cleared her throat and continued. "You wanted this hot wife, not a family. Was it her idea, getting pregnant? Did she coerce you in some way? Spend too much? Did she withhold sex from you or trick you in some way, maybe? Stop taking the pill?"

Davenport eyed her steadily. He did not rise, he did not bark. He simply and deliberately reached a finger over to his phone and pressed a button. In no less than a few seconds, two security guards entered the office from a secret door hidden in the wood paneled wall.

"The detectives will be leaving now," he said to the men, all the while staring directly at Eisen. "Please show them the way out."

He rose from his desk once the security guards were situated behind the detectives.

"It's reassuring that our fair city has the two of you to look after it," Davenport mocked. "I will be speaking with the commissioner about this. Do have a nice day."

"We can come back with a warrant," Eisen threatened as she turned to challenge Davenport.

"That is exactly what it will take."

Once out on the street, Eisen grabbed her partner, who was making a bee line for the unmarked car.

"Wait."

"Food," Erikson intoned in a zombie like voice, "Me hungry."

"That can wait. What do you make of him?"

"He's an asshole; a pissed off, angry, asshole who lost a shit load of money."

"He's got to be insured."

"Of course, but com'on, Deb, do you really think it's about the money with him? It's got to be a big blow to the ego. No one steps up to someone like him and does something like that without incurring his wrath."

"Hence the corporate bulldogs."

"Oh, he's got to have someone working this case from the inside, private security, private this, private that. Can we go eat, please?"

"You think he's hiding something?"

"Everybody's hiding something."

"Tell me."

"For real?"

"Yeah."

"Then we can go eat?"

"Sure."

"Yes, he's pissed about the money, not that it's gone, but that someone could take it from him that easily. No way is he thinking this kid is getting healed. Maybe he figures it's a scam, this guy has got to have been targeted before. You don't make that kind of money without drawing attention to yourself."

"But what of the actual healing?"

"There was no healing."

"Bear with me, just check this out, let's say this kid was healed. Let's say he gets up and moves and breathes on his own. Wouldn't this guy be moved, even just for a minute? Wouldn't something like that make this guy believe?"

"Maybe he's seen this kind of parlor trick before."

"I'm not talking Billy Graham, bam, you're healed here, Mark. What if it was something more?"

"OK, I'll bite; what if what you say is true? What if a healing took place? The kid walks, everybody is happy, whoop-de-fucking-doo. Then why does this miracle maker have to break into someone's house? Why does he go to the trouble of holding someone ransom? Wouldn't you think that someone doing good deeds wouldn't be going about it in a bad way?"

"That's what doesn't make sense."

"If," Erikson said, "we were talking miracles, which we are not."

"Yes, but…"

"Oh come on, please! I'm starving! Let's eat. I promise you can talk until you're blue in the face about this, but I have to eat!"

After they ate, after they discussed the case until Eisen grew tired and after he dropped her off at her apartment, Erikson found himself not tired enough for sleep. Rather than going home and watching the TV while drinking beer like he told himself he should, he found himself driving the streets.

He drove around for hours until he came upon what he was looking for. He pulled the car up next to the young woman with the see-through top and parked. She looked at him through the windshield with uncertainty. She wasn't afraid, but she wasn't feeling at ease.

Erikson lowered the passenger window and motioned for her to come closer. She approached hesitantly and peeked inside the window. Erikson could see through her top; the cold night air making her nipples erect.

"Get in," he said.

Chapter 12

That evening, long after Detective Deborah Eisen walked through her front door of her apartment, after she slid her firearm into the thumb print gun safe in the top drawer of her night stand, the safe she no longer needed, after she mixed herself a few drinks, after she fell asleep on the couch, she found herself awake once again, standing in the short hallway that led to the apartment's two small bedrooms. She had been sleep walking again, but rather than finding herself suddenly awake in the shower, fully clothed, or in the kitchen smearing peanut butter on a steak and attempting to jam it into the toaster, she found herself outside her daughter's bedroom.

She found her hand on the door knob. She could not recall if she was leaving the room or entering it. She took her hand away then touched the knob again. It felt warm in her hand, but she reasoned that she could have been standing here in this pose for hours. She turned the knob and pushed the door open. She caught her breath and stepped into the room, closing the door behind her but not turning on the light. She leaned back against the door, eyes closed, despite being in darkness, save for the daggers of light that the semi drawn Venetian blinds surrendered.

She knew this room by heart, knew where the bed was, the dresser, the area rug with all the jungle animals on it. She knew all the animals, too, by name even; Lioney, the lion, Tigey the tiger, Ellie the elephant. She found herself laughing at the simple names the animals were given. She felt that laughter echo off into brittle notes that led to a tremor deep inside her and to keep it from spreading. She dug her heel hard against the bottom of the door until she winced in pain.

She walked softly on tiptoes, so as not to wake anyone who might be sleeping. She made her way to the bed and knelt down beside it. She could almost make out the shallow breaths, and she could smell the sweetness. She lifted the covers, careful not to disturb, and slid into the bed, pulling the covers only as much as they'd be willing to give. She let her head rest on the pillow and lay still, trying to hear the creaking, the breathing, and the life that was once so much a part of this room.

She inched her head ever slowly as she let the tears come, rubbing her face against the satin princess pillow in an attempt to keep from crying, twisting her face deeper into the fabric, trying to stop. She inhaled and at once knew the familiar scent she had not forgotten, that she could never forget.

The tremors returned, not wholly unwelcome, challenging her breathing until she felt as if she'd suffocate.

The part of her, deep down, the one that was lost and alone wanted this. She wanted to let go, to stop the pain, the hurt, and worst of all, the unfathomable emptiness that ripped at her heart from missing her daughter.

She was trembling now, shaking, and forcing her face deeper into the pillow until it finally came for her. She lifted slightly off the bed and howled, the scream of hurt and pain and anger. She clenched the sheets in her fists, first tugging at them, then finally bringing them against her temples in an attempt to make all of this go away, thinking that the pressure she could exert against her brain would make it stop, yet knowing full well that it never would.

This was almost a nightly ritual. She'd find herself at the door and hope beyond hope that things were different, that bad things never happened, that her daughter was asleep behind this door.

But this night was different. This night when she passed out, instead of waking up numb, she woke feeling something she had not felt in such a long time.

Last night, she dreamt for the first time. Any dream was a blessing, a distraction from the pain. But this dream was different, was better than any she could have hoped for.

She dreamt of her daughter.

And she remembered it, as she woke, moving slowly, trying to stay asleep, trying to delay the inevitable, unwelcome morning. She wanted to stay there, she wanted to be there.

She saw her daughter's face, animated again with life. She was smiling, a grand smile, framing the remnants of a beautiful laugh. They were playing in the park, chasing each other, laughing and when caught, tickling each other. She chased her daughter around a willow tree, ducking under the weeping branches, reaching for her and grabbing nothing but leaves.

77

"Mommy, I can't see you!"

"I can see you!"

And just when Deb would reach out to catch her, she'd be gone, her hands clutching at air that held nothing but the laughter of her child.

When she finally caught her, she pulled her down on top of her, tickling her wildly, until the squeals of joy came rushing out of her, her breath holding the fragrance of flowers.

"Mommy?"

"Yes, lovely?"

"Are you ok?"

"Of course, dear."

"I'm worried about you."

"Me?"

"Yes."

"But why sweetheart?"

"You look like you've been crying."

"It's the tickles."

"Tickles make you sad?"

"Tickles make me cry, but in a good way."

"I miss this park, mommy. I wish we could go here more."

"So do I."

"Hey, guess what mommy!"

"What sweetie?"

"I made a new friend."

"Oh you did?"

"Yes."

"He lives here in the park."

"Oh, that's lovely! What kind of animal is he?"

"Oh, he's not an animal. He's a man. He lives in the trunk of the oak tree, but only sometimes."

"Is he nice?"

"Yes, but he never, ever smiles."

"That's too bad."

"Can you see him, mommy?"

Deborah looked across the park at the old oak tree. She tried to pick out this man of which her daughter spoke, but couldn't.

"No, sweetie, I can't."

"There he is," she said pointing.

Eisen stood up and scanned the park, seeing nothing as far as the eye could see. At last, she noticed a slight man, walking toward the tree. He walked quickly, his head bend down and his fists dug forcefully into his pockets, pulling his overcoat tight around him. She noticed that he was wearing the ski mask described to her by Janine Davenport.

She waved to him, but he took no notice. Deborah stood up and waved both arms, but no notice was taken. She began calling out to the man, but was surprised that her voice made no sound. She screamed, yet no sound came. She turned to her daughter in desperation, but she had vanished. The tree, the sad and lonely weeping willow that they sat under was gone. The park had just dissolved into nothing but green grass for miles and that one oak tree.

She tried to run towards the tree, hoping to cut him off, but found her legs not working correctly; they hitched and jerked out to the sides instead of in a fluid back and forth motion. She stumbled and fell, got back up, and stumbled and fell again. The breath in her throat, feeling it for the first time, was hot and dry. She reached out, trying in vain for contact, but found none.

She scrambled to her feet just in time to see the man disappear behind the door. She struggled to run and finally, as if shaking off some invisible restraint, she sprinted, legs working beautifully now.

She reached the door and began banging desperately on it. She found, just like her voice, that her fists made no sound when they made contact with the wooden door. She kept hitting it, and with each successive blow she heard a faint noise, like the volume of a TV set in the next room. She banged more and more, finally heard the sound coming from her fists, getting louder and louder.

She heard footsteps coming closer behind the door. Still she kept banging and just as the doorknob was turning, just as she felt a wave of lightness, maybe hope even, she shot upright in bed. She noticed her lungs heaving, desperate for air, as if she had surfaced from deep waters.

The banging continued. She finally realized that she was in her daughter's room, she had fallen asleep here.

"Coming, I'm coming," she yelled to quell the banging. It stopped. She retrieved her house coat from the bathroom and rushed to the door. She straightened her hair best she could and without looking through the peephole, swung the door open.

"What?" She demanded.

"You look like shit," her partner replied.

"Nice to see you, too."

She walked away from the open door, leaving Erikson standing in the doorway holding two coffees.

"May I come in?"

She ignored him as he stood there. She sat down in a chair facing the window that overlooked the park; concrete surface and sparse grass, the opposite of her dream.

"Am I interrupting something," he asked, "I mean, I can come back. Or if I can be of any assistance…"

"Come, go, whatever."

"I'll come in then. I brought you a coffee."

He crossed the living room and handed her the coffee. She absentmindedly reached for it, mumbled a soft thanks and took a sip.

"Got a cigarette?"

"Deb, you don't smoke."

"Are we gonna do this again? I asked you for a cigarette. I know you got 'em."

He reached into the inside pocket of his jacket and pulled out the packet of cigarettes and handed them to her. She took notice of the item she received this time, turning it over and over in her hand.

"So, these are those fancy cigarettes Janine Davenport seemed so impressed with, huh?"

"Same old, same old."

"I think she likes you."

"I doubt that."

"Fancy cigarettes, nice suit."

"I don't think I'm her type."

"Young and handsome."

"Not rich."

"Yeah, well I can sense a huge divorce settlement coming up for her, so I think the next guy will be more your type."

"Well, she's not my type."

Eisen sensed his irritability with this and decided to drop it.

"Got a light?"

He reached into his pocket and pulled out a lighter. He struck it, reached it under her cigarette and held it there while she pulled on it, making the embers burn red.

"Rough night, huh?"

She nodded her head as she blew a long stream of grey smoke from her lungs. She looked at the cigarette between the index and middle finger of her right hand. She brought her hand to her face and rubbed her thumb deep into her right eye socket, forcing her lids closed, until the bright room blurred into darkness.

Erikson pulled a loose cigarette from the pack and lit up. He smoked in silence along side her for a moment, wondering if she was going to say anything, offer anything up.

"I know you don't want to talk about it," he said, breaking the standoff and the silence, "maybe not to me, but you need to talk to someone. I know you don't talk to the shrink; it doesn't take a genius to figure that one out. But talk to someone, please, anyone, a priest even for fuck's sake."

She turned to acknowledge him and Erikson thought maybe she was going to say something. Instead, she blew a column of smoke in his direction. She ground out the stub, watching him through the haze of smoke.

"I'm going to take a shower," she announced and stood up in front of him, her robe opening slightly, her womanhood revealed. She then rolled her shoulders slowly and the robe fell to the floor, a swath of silk wound around her.

Wow, Erikson thought, she looked good. She was in great shape for a woman her age. Most woman he encountered, even in their twenties that never had kids didn't look this good. And the ones that became moms did so with the remains of the baby fat from a pregnancy never fully gone away.

Her body was beyond amazing. It was her skin, her level of fitness, her curves that just being there in front of him, naked that was causing Erikson to become uncomfortable. He longed for this, dreamt of it, to be before her, to be offered her gift of sex. But not like this.

She stared down at Erikson, eyes moist with the tears that were yet to fall. He desired to reach out and touch her, to run his fingers along the inside of her thigh, upwards until he could hear her breathing deepen. Then he'd pull her towards him and touch her with his tongue, tasting her essence. Yet all he could do was look away. He made a conscious effort not to stare at her still firm breasts, the cold air of morning making the nipples hard and erect. He looked down, past her flat stomach and once he realized that he was looking at the trimmed crop of hair between her legs, he looked away from her completely.

When he looked up at her, he found that she was no longer looking at him. She was staring straight ahead, staring at nothing.

His mouth was dry. He wanted to say something, but no words were created for this moment. He wanted to reach up and take her hand in his and tell her it was ok, that everything would be fine, but he found himself motionless. He felt paralyzed, felt stranded in a body that could never know how to do the right thing before a woman like this.

She stepped over the robe and walked towards the bathroom. Erikson noticed the cigarette in his left hand, still burning. The ash was almost an inch long now. He took a sip of his coffee to wet his mouth and finished off the cigarette in one long drag. He then dropped the remains of it into his coffee, swirling it around after the hiss.

He got up and noticed that the bathroom door was not closed. He heard the water running, saw her moving about, still naked. His loins ached and he felt delirious. He wanted to feel himself inside her and the lust he felt was now overwhelming. He decided to follow her into the bathroom and take her.

He would walk in behind her and find her standing with her back to him. He knew this from the first step he

83

took. He would then place his left hand so gently around her left breast, caressing her skin before pulling softly at her nipple with his fingers. He would place his right hand on her head and pull her against him. He would let his fingers massage her scalp as he placed his lips so close to her neck that she could feel his breath. He would then, ever so slightly, brush his lips against her neck before finally kissing her.

He would then free his right and hand and place it on her stomach. He would not linger here, but move directly down towards the sweetness between her legs. There he would explore with his fingers; sliding, rubbing, penetrating. He would work her into a frenzy before guiding her towards the sink, positioning her as he wanted, slowly free himself from his pants and put himself inside her.

As he neared the bathroom, he could see her bedroom at the end of the short hall. As he got closer, he could see her bed, still made, without even the slightest impression that someone had crashed on the covers.

Across from the bathroom was the other bedroom and he noticed that this door was open. What distracted him away from his resolve was that this door was never open. All the times he had been here, it was closed. Even the times when he used her bathroom, he would check the handle, only to find it always locked.

Distracted now, he slowly leaned his head into the doorway and noticed that this was her daughter's room. The toys, all neatly placed, gave the impression that this room was more like those rooms at IKEA, the scenery for what life could be like if you had a repressed, Swedish child who inspired to be a great, modern architect. Like Eisen's bedroom, there was no sign that a child actually lived here.

Not that he thought she'd pack things up, but the manner in which she held out against obvious conclusions puzzled him.

She refused to talk about it. One would think, he thought, that you'd want to talk, want to hear yourself talk about it, hear her name pass your lips, resonate in the air and caress your thoughts. Loved ones are always there, Erikson recalled his grandmother once saying, if you breathe life into their memory by speaking of them, and in times of despair, to them.

He could understand her rage, of course. But her unwillingness to let others in, to let them share the burden of her grief, was beginning to wear on those around her. Certainly, police take care of their own and when something like this hits one of them, it hits them all. However, her distance and her own desire to exclude anyone from the grief, from any of the burden, was beginning to cause friction.

Yet Erikson was patient, had stayed her partner, even if, in his mind, he was on the periphery. He gave her the space she needed, but decided he would never give up on helping her. Sure, every inquiry was met with hostility, but he could understand. He knew loss. While hers was a child, his own father was a policeman and his life was cut short by the perils of the profession. He knew the cavern that was created inside when someone you love, someone you count on, will never be coming home again.

Forgetting the bathroom and his desire, he passed the threshold and paused before the bed. As he got closer, he noticed that the princess themed comforter and pillows were in disarray. They weren't messy like someone had pulled down the comforter and tossed about the sheets. A large person had obviously laid down here, whether or not the intention was to sleep here or grieve. He knew she wanted to feel her daughter, feel her warmth and hear her breath as she slept. She was tough, but Erikson knew that beneath her tough exterior she was hurting, and he was worried for her.

He pulled at the comforter, grabbing an edge and straightened it. He pulled it up to the head of the bed and placed the pillows in a neat fashion on top. He then picked up the three stuffed animals that lay on the floor beside the bed and arranged them the best he could into a happy threesome of friends. He starred at the arrangement, wondering if he did a decent job, wondered just for a moment what kind of father he would be. At the very least, he thought, he could make a bed, maybe even tuck someone in, read a bedtime story, kiss a boo boo and wipe tears away. But the crying and messiness, would he be able to handle that?

A creak behind him brought him back to the present. He turned to see Deborah standing there watching him. How long she had been there, he didn't know. He tried to take note of when the shower stopped, but he had clearly missed it.

She stood there, hugging herself in a towel wrapped around her, covering her nakedness. Her hair shiny, dripping wet, tucked behind her ears. She was silent, her lips quivering, as she stood staring at Erikson.

"Thank you."

She then abruptly turned back to the hall. He could hear her footsteps on the bare wood floor as she made her way to her bedroom. Before he could follow, before he could even move, he heard the click of the latch as she closed the door. He had no recourse; she was gone again, back to her defenses, and he had little hope of her becoming vulnerable again.

Chapter 13

"Why are we here?"

Slava turned quickly and grabbed Donovan by the lapel of his jacket and pulled him close as they crept from the bushes towards the gate. The fact that this action caused Donovan's head to bang off the heavy gate, to Slava, was a bonus. Crouching there, he held a finger up to his mouth signaling for him to shut up.

"OK," he now whispered, "sorry."

"Shhh," Slava replied, "no talking."

"Why are we being so quiet? There's no one here!"

"Shhh, security always here."

"You've got to be kidding me!"

Slava turned to Donovan again, but this time punched him hard in the chest. Donovan buckled from the blow and fell to his knees.

"I tell you shut up, you shut up," he whispered forcefully.

Slava went to picking the lock and ignored Donovan's quiet grunts of pain. He worked quickly now, unimpeded by the young priest's inquiries and soon had the padlock open and was silently removing the heavy chain that kept the heavy wooden, wrought iron reinforced gates locked.

Slava pulled at one of the gates and, while dragging Donovan along the gravel drive, created an opening large enough for the black sedan to slip through. He then pulled the gate to within three feet of being closed. He looked at Donovan, who was finally getting to his feet again.

"Are you coming?"

Donovan dusted himself off and hobbled through the opening as Slava pulled the gate closed.

"You mind telling me now, where are we?"

"Secret."

"A secret? This is a secret? You have got to be kidding me!"

"Come, we must hurry."

Slava and Donovan ran until they caught up to the black sedan, parked under a grove of trees, almost invisible on this moonless night. Crispis leaned against the hood, smoking a cigarette. Without looking and without asking, he produced a cigarette for Slava and lit it from his own. Slava took it directly from the driver's hands into his mouth. He inhaled deeply and exhaled quietly.

"You look tired," Crispis said mockingly.

"Is long way," replied the Russian.

"You know," Crispis said, "you can tell how much money someone has by how far it is to their house from the main road."

"How far?"

"Three quarters of a mile!"

"Good," Slava said, pausing to inhale on his cigarette, "will be good tonight."

"Who is it," asked Donovan.

"We don't know," answered Crispis.

"Aren't you curious?"

"No. It doesn't matter. One is as good as the next."

Donovan kicked the toe of his boot back and forth at the edge of the gravel drive, and mumbled something under his breath.

"Sorry, I didn't get that," Crispis responded.

"If these people are so well off," he repeated louder this time, "they'd have a paved driveway.

"No, pavement no good," Slava countered.

"He's right," Crispis added, "pavement is quiet. If you have the kind of money these people must have, you want something that will tip you off when someone is coming. Cameras are good, but they can be beaten, as I'm sure Mac has already done, but nothing beats a good old fashioned crunchy, noisy gravel drive."

"What about dogs," Donovan challenged.

"Depends on what kind of dog you're talking about; guard dogs or personal protection dogs," Crispis countered.

"What's the difference?"

"Territory. Guard dogs are not command controlled, unlike personal protection dogs. Guard dogs sense your presence and like a missile, they lock on. They're bad news."

"And the other are better," Donovan asked sarcastically.

"Well, yeah. The owner can call off a protection dog. You ever seen a guard dog get called off?"

"Hauled off you, maybe," Slava added.

"But no worries, these people have neither. They put all their faith into modern electronics. Such a waste of money, but that's rich people."

"Da, should have had dog, big dog," Slava said approvingly.

"Hold up," Crispis said, making a fist and holding it up for them to be quiet. He pulled out his cell and found a text from Mac.

"We're all set. Let's go."

As they approached the house, the overly large and overly ornate door swung open. Mac was grinning, which was his custom, but tonight he had never smiled so readily.

"Evening, gentlemen. May I get your coats?"

"Mac, where's your mask?"

"Oh, Crispis, this one is truly a blessing. This guy's blind."

"No family? Where's the family?"

"In Aspen."

"No, they supposed to be here."

"Well, they ain't."

"Something ain't right," Crispis hesitated. "This guy ain't supposed to be blind."

"Well, if it makes you feel any better, it will be easier for Judas to do what he do" Mac countered, smiling even more before adding, "and as an added bonus, we're already in the safe."

Chapter 14

Crispis reached his hand deep into the safe and still his hand did not reach the back of it. For what his hand did reach, it fell upon many stacks and as he pulled it out, along came four straps of bills. He saw that he was holding forty thousand dollars in his right hand. He dropped the straps into a bag and reached in again.

"Sixteen million," Mac beamed, "all nice and neat in tightly wrapped bricks."

"Who keeps this much cash in a safe," Crispis asked. "I can see a few mil, but com'on now, this ain't right."

"Right as rain," Mac answered.

"What do you think Slava?"

"A lot of money to keep in house."

"Donovan?"

"I don't know, Crispis, I never saw a few million before I started hanging with you fellas, so maybe sixteen million isn't out of the question."

Crispis pulled a brick out of the safe and let it drop to the floor. He nodded to Slava who, understanding fully what he meant, pulled out his large knife and cut into the plastic shrink wrap. He pulled off the protective skin and pushed the neat stack over. The inside straps slid out from under, disfiguring the large cube, and spilled over Slava's boots. They were blank.

Crispis swore under his breath, and then looked up at Mac, then at Donovan.

"What I tell you? This shit ain't right."

Slava gently moved Crispis aside then began violently ripping the bricks out of the safe, throwing the cubes left and right in a frenzy of motion. After all the currency was removed, Slava, still outraged, kicked at the back wall of the safe. His boots struck solid metal, but they caused an echo. Surprised, he turned and looked at Crispis, who nodded back and then smiled.

"I'll be damned," Crispis said, "a safe within a safe. Gentlemen, start looking, there should be a switch here somewhere to activate this door. I don't see any hinge or latch, so I'm guessing it's a slider and most likely power activated."

The men began ripping the room apart, tearing books off shelves, pictures off walls, everything that could hide a switch or a button. They broke furniture, tore apart books, broke sculptures, broke open everything they could, yet they found no means of egress into whatever was behind the safe.

"Mac," Crispis said, sitting down wearily against the wall, "can we blow it open?"

"No, it's too thick. Besides, I don't have enough plastic for a proper job and if I had enough, that much would bring the house down."

"Fuck," yelled Slava in desperation, "now what?"

"Donovan," Crispis directed, "go find Judas. Tell him the situation and tell him we need the man of the house to open this for us. Go now."

Donovan ran off to look for Judas. Mac shook his head wistfully, avoiding the 'I told you so' look Crispis could rightly be wearing. It had never happened this way before, he thought. It was always so easy, so uncomplicated. They find a mark, study him, find all his assets and net worth, then when the time is right, they begin the operation. Easy in, easy out.

What made it actually enjoyable was that they were able to give more than they took. They had something to offer that rendered all their worldly possessions, millions of dollars, patents, stock options, rare art, diamonds and artifacts worthless. They could offer something in return for all that. They had the answer for what these people secretly prayed for. They could fulfill the prayers made in the dark of night, in the cold shade of a pale winter, prayers which God himself would never grant. Judas could heal, could undo whatever ills the body had become heir to. He could undo the injustice of a cruel God.

Slava whipped out his .45 and aimed it at the door. Crispis quickly put his hand on Slava's arm and made him lower the weapon. He shook his head at the Russian's idea.

"Ricochet, Slava. You wanna get hit?"

"Nyet. I just want to get fucking door open."

"Me too, man, me too. Hey Mac, how much we got, just them straps on top?"

"Bottom too, Crispis, all told we got twelve thousand, eight hundred."

93

"Shit," Crispis responded, "that ain't nothing."

He leaned hard against the wall and kicked over a stack of books that was piled on the floor. He bent his knees and just as gravity had played upon the books, Crispis soon was sitting on the floor. He looked up and watched as Slava lit a smoke and exhaled heavily.

"Lots of books here," Slava said as he exhaled.

"This man has a massive library, that's true," Crispis agreed as he reached a blind hand above his head and pulled out a book. He let the tomb fall into his lap and studied it for a moment.

"War and Peace. Hmm. You read this, Slava?"

"Nyet."

"This is a Russian classic, no? And it ain't like you ain't got the time."

Slava ignored this comment and sat, extending his long legs. He focused his attention on his right boot, rotating it left and right and back again, as if making sure it would work properly if the sudden need to stand up should occur. He then tapped the ash of his cigarette into the palm of his left hand, being respectful of the obviously expensive carpeting, despite recklessly trashing the room just moments before.

"Chekhov," Slava said.

"Hmm?"

"Chekhov. I like Chekhov. As child, I sneak into theatre. Not difficult; break into building next door through basement, climb to roof, jump parapet,..."

"Typical Slava style," Mac beamed.

"Da! I find seat and watch. What else to do, was freezing outside."

He dragged wistfully on his cigarette and starred up at the tinned ceiling for a good minute or two.

"Was beautiful," he added quietly.

Mac smiled at Slava's sentimentality. It contrasted so starkly with his personality; brusque, silent and deadly. Mac tried to picture Slava as a youth and found it impossible. He couldn't picture him as a child, couldn't get a sense of him ever bring vulnerable, ever being dependent on someone. He tried to separate the man from the child and clinging to his last comment, tried to reconcile a tender side of a child who finds beauty in a work of art with the coldness of the adult he has grown into.

He was fond of Slava. He felt compassion towards him, despite the manner in which they found him. He often thought about that day, more often when Slava would survive situations where he felt, in all probability, he would perish. He was tough, he was strong and he was cruel. When Mac thought of Slava, he thought too of why Judas had chosen him. He knew Judas had a reason, had a plan and he never thought to question it. Not out of respect, rather he would often see the brilliance in Judas' strategies. But Slava was different, for a number of reasons.

So that day, well over a hundred years ago, when he and Judas came upon Slava still hanging from the rope meant to end his life, Mac found it curious that he wouldn't die. They watched from a hilltop as his body jerked and fought when the horse he was seated on was slapped away. They watched as he fought, trying in vain to free his hands. They watched as his face turned red, then white. They watched the crowd of villagers taunt him and cheer his death and they watched as one by one, over the course of many hours, the villagers became afraid and crossed themselves as Slava refused to die.

After the last of the superstitious peasants fled in horror, crossing themselves and muttering prayers, Judas and Mac revealed themselves to him. Judas offered and Slava, as well as he could communicate with the noose choking him, accepted.

Now Mac found himself wondering how a child who found beauty in a play could end up as he did. Mac looked across at Crispis, still paging through War & Peace, when a thought struck him.

"Crispis?"

"Hmmmm," he answered without looking up.

"Where's that young priest of ours? He should have been back by now."

Crispis shot ramrod straight and slapped the book shut with his left hand while his right hand brought up his radio.

"Donovan? Donovan?"

"Shhhh, listen," Mac interrupted with a wave of his hand.

They froze for a moment and waited for what Mac had alluded to; footsteps coming towards them at a rapid pace. Slava, forgetting the respect he had shown moments earlier, ground out his cigarette on the carpet and from the strength of his legs, pushed himself up the wall, leaving his hands free to produce a .45 in each clenched fist. He slid quickly towards the doorway and then swung his body into the opening, ready to fire.

Donovan let out a yelp as he ducked to avoid the ready gun and slammed into the jamb across from Slava, falling awkwardly into the room.

"He's gone," Donovan managed, between gulps of breath.

"What, who's gone?"

"Judas! He's gone!"

At that moment, the rear of the safe let out a click and slid quickly into the wall, leaving an opening to what should have been a secret room. Instead, they were looking

96

outside onto what could have been a courtyard or a garden, bathed in ever increasing white light.

The brilliant light coming from that room made them forget, for an instance, about the money and about their missing compatriot.

"Is that…" Mac began, stunned.

"Close your eyes," Crispis screamed. "Don't look at it!"

Slava almost fell forward, reaching instead for a bookcase to steady himself, eyes shut tight.

"Oh my God," was the last thing they heard Donovan say.

Chapter 15

"Punch it!"

Detective Eisen rapped impatiently at the passenger window, keeping rhythm with the rain as it fell.

"Com'on, let's go," she added.

"I'm going, ok, ease up. Conditions aren't the greatest," Erikson replied. "You know, we probably shouldn't be doing this. No, we definitely shouldn't be doing this."

"It was called in."

"They called in a 602 with a 901h."

"Yeah, trespasser on scene; possible dead body; request an ambulance."

"And that sounds like our case?"

"Yes."

"We should at least wait for a patrol car to respond first, wait until they call us in."

"Given the way you drive, it would take the same amount of time."

Erikson shook his head and managed a terse smile.

"Give me one good reason why you think it's one of ours?"

"I can feel it."

"You can feel it? Or is it just wishful thinking? It could have been any smash and grab."

"Com'on, Mark, have some faith. It's at the coordinating intersection of Monaco and Lisbon Boulevard? No house near there under two million. It's our boys."

Erikson pushed the Crown Vic as fast as he dared in this weather. The beating rain couldn't drown out the annoying rapping sound Eisen made. Even worse, it couldn't distract him from thinking about procedure and how much trouble they could be in. He cared deeply about his partner and worried for her, even when he knew she wasn't thinking clearly. He knew he'd eventually have to make a decision; probably sooner than he'd like. He'd have to go all in, whole hog and side with his partner as one would expect, or step aside in favor of what was up to this point a very promising career. He knew though that each option cancelled the other out. He couldn't be a good partner by walking away; his sense of loyalty was too strong for that. He just hoped that something would give; something would cause her to back down, just for a moment, and see things as he did.

"Relax, I'm right about this," her voice broke in, almost as if responding to his thoughts, "I can feel it."

"Alright," he heard himself say, "maybe it is and maybe not. Worst thing that can happen is that we pick up another case right?"

"That's right."

"So much for no overtime."

"Com'on, Mark, is there anywhere else you'd rather be than right here, right now, chasing a hot lead?"

He looked at Eisen and saw some semblance of her old self. He smiled to himself and added silently that there was no one else he'd rather be with as well.

Chapter 16

"You certainly have a flair for the dramatic," Judas admitted.

"I thought a little flourish was in order, given the circumstances," Jesus replied.

"It's been a long time."

"Yes it has."

"And you decide to show up now?"

"It's time."

"I suppose it is," Judas thought, eyeing his old friend suspiciously. The cut of the clothes was modern, befitting the times, but he couldn't get over the short hair, the clean shaven look. "So, what do you want?"

"To save the world, same as you," Jesus said.

"You think that's what I want?"

"Isn't it?"

"Oh, for pity's sake! Is it the clothes, or were you always this sanctimonious?!"

"Well, I thought a more modern look was apropos. I do like these suits they wear nowadays. That Tom Ford, I must find a way to Saint him."

"At least you haven't lost your sense of humor."

"One tends to need it in my line of work."

"Nice touch too, bringing me here, to this garden," Judas said. "Kind of reminds me of the last time I saw you; in the Garden of Gethsemane. Nice sense of symmetry."

"Thank you," Jesus said with a bow.

"You know," Judas paused as he searched carefully for the right words, "by all rights I should hate you."

"Hate me? Why?"

"Why?!?! You condemn me to this unending torture!"

"I saved you."

"You call this salvation? Living a life that will not end?"

"It was the only way to save you."

"Well, you kinda screwed that one up, huh?"

"Judas, the Father did not know of our plan, could not know."

"So all that 'forgive them Father, they know not what they do' business didn't include me?"

"Someone had to betray me to fulfill the prophecy."

"All things considered, I would have had you make Peter do it?"

"He was too weak."

"And the others? The famed Matthew, Mark, Luke and John? Why not them?"

"They had to tell the story."

"Was I not loyal, Jesus? Did I not love thee?"

"Yes, you were loyal above all others; your love the most pure."

"Then why?"

"For that same reason, Judas. It was you and could only be you."

"The pain it caused me, the sickness, and the regret."

"You had to do it."

"You have no idea of the pain."

"Indeed, even upon the cross, I felt it."

"Then why not let me die when I chose?"

"The Kingdom of Heaven could never be yours if I had allowed you to take your own life."

"And the alternative to this could have been worse?"

"Judas, please understand why I did what I did. My death was not the end, it was only the beginning. I gave you the power to heal yourself, so that you could never die."

"I'd trade it all for my name not to be vilified!"

"No, you cannot mean that. I gave you the gift to heal! Such a wonderful gift!"

"A curse," Judas countered. "Jesus, I am tired, so very tired. I just want this all to end."

"It will."

"How?"

"The end is nigh, my friend. But, for every ending, there is a beginning. And you shall have a say in that."

"Speak plainly," Judas said, again sounding irritated.

"I am here as it was prophesied. I am here to usher in the end of days. But not end of all days; the end of the old and the beginning of the new. However, I cannot do it alone. As it once was and again shall be; I seek your assistance."

"And if I refuse?"

"The world will end."

"Why do you do this, Jesus? Why do you torment me so? Is it not enough I sacrificed everything for you? What more will you have me endure? I am tired, my soul exhausted. I feel pain, not just in my body, but in my heart. And if I must speak honestly, the pain in my heart still holds in bloom anger towards you. I have been forsaken by an act of your choosing. 'Betray me Judas, you must, it is the only way!' You say I was the only one, the strongest one, the purest one. And what did I seek? Merely to live by your word, to stand by your side and share your love. And by that word, did salvation come? No. Was I offered forgiveness? No. I was condemned to this life by a 'gift' that you so generously bestowed upon me. And for what? For what purpose?"

"That will remain to be seen."

"You know, had you come a thousand years ago, five hundred, perhaps even a century ago, I may have relented. I may have welcomed you and fallen upon my knees and kissed your feet. But not only was I forsaken, I was forgotten. Why have you not responded to me Jesus? I have prayed to you, yet still you shun me."

"You have not been forsaken."

"Then why?" Judas demanded.

"How much has been written of my love? How many Scriptures must be read over and over in the churches, the prisons, the death beds or in the private moments? What more can be said? I must let my children live their lives by my word, let them live freely and have them choose to be right by me. Those that do are granted the riches and those that do not are still offered a chance at redemption. Like a parent to a child, I must step aside and let them choose for themselves."

"Then let me choose!"

"Judas, don't you see? There is a reason for

everything, and a reason for why I need you. You and you alone can do what finally needs to be done."

Judas turned his back on Jesus and walked to the remnants of a fallen tree and sat. His body felt heavier than in recent weeks. He felt weak, sick and nauseous. His heart ached; he felt the pain as the love he never lost wrestled with the hatred that all these years had bestowed upon him.

"I'm sorry, Jesus," he said wearily, "I will not help you."

Jesus at first appeared wounded by this, and then he offered Judas a smile that held no ill will.

"I shall see you again, very soon, my friend. I have faith that you will reconsider. I know you Judas, I know your heart."

And then he was gone, once again like before, leaving Judas alone in the garden, but this time, too exhausted for tears.

Chapter 17

Much to Erikson's relief, they arrived at the scene well after the responding patrol cars. As they had gotten closer, he radioed in a response, so he felt better about their situation. He turned the car into the drive and stopped.

"There's a house here?"

"Mansion," Eisen corrected.

"Yeah, but I don't see anything."

"Then they gotta be loaded, the rich of the rich."

"How can you tell?"

"You don't watch a whole lot of daytime TV, do you?"

"I don't really find the time," Erikson said.

"OK, a really good signifier of wealth is how long your driveway is. Given that you probably drive twenty-five miles an hour on a driveway, you can figure the distance based on how long it takes to get to the front door."

"Are you serious?"

"It's simple math."

"Whatever," he sighed and started the car up the drive. After several minutes, they came over the crest of a hill that opened to a large courtyard that led to a monstrous house beyond. He pulled up and parked next to the three responding patrol cars.

"Look!"

Erikson turned and followed where Eisen was pointing. There, across the courtyard, up on a grassy knoll, was parked an ambulance. The paramedics were loading somebody on a gurney into the vehicle.

"I'm going."

"What? Wait," Erikson called out after his partner, who was heading towards the ambulance.

"You cover the scene," she called back without breaking stride. "I'll meet you at the hospital later."

Erikson watched as his partner reached the paramedics, spoke briefly with the driver, then disappeared in the back. The lights came on and the ambulance slowly crept off the lawn and onto the drive, where it then broke out the sirens and sped off. Though out of sight now, Erikson could still see the lights reflected off the trees that lined the drive as it left the property.

"OK boys," he said to two patrolmen standing outside as he approached the massive covered entry, "what do we have here?"

Father Donovan's head was pounding. All he could hear were murmurs and brittle noises, like pins dropping and echoing. The hushed tones that he began to think might be conversations became abrasive to him; each sound like metal upon metal, scratching and grinding.

He still couldn't see, so he had no idea if he were awake or dreaming. But he did become aware of his breathing, which was becoming rapid now. He could vaguely sense his body and begin to feel pressures on it. He couldn't move and the frightening sounds began getting closer. He thought he was struggling to move, to avoid these sounds, but his body wouldn't respond. The sounds he so feared kept coming closer until they were almost inside him, echoing in his brain.

Then silence.

What Donovan first noticed when he regained consciousness was the smell of coffee. He had once been a big drinker; sometimes drinking as many as eight cups a day. But he saw it as a vice that temptation wrought and banished it from his life. He missed the taste of a strong cup of black coffee, but he could get by without it. But now the smell was overwhelming. As he inhaled deeply, he heard a sound, as if someone was shifting a chair.

"Who's there?"

He tried to see, but everything was dark. He slowly touched his eyes to see if they were covered but found nothing there.

"The lights, please," he managed hoarsely.

"They're on," an unfamiliar voice said.

"Who are you? Where am I?"

"You're safe. You're in a hospital."

"Are you a nurse?"

"No, but I was told to call for one should you awake."

Donovan struggled to sit up, but found his movements useless.

108

"I can't move. Why can't I move?"

"I don't know. You're not restrained, so it could be some meds they gave you. Here," the voice trailed off as he felt the bed on which he lay shudder and begin to move him to a seated position.

"Now then," the voice began, getting closer.

"Why can't I see?"

"Don't know and it's really not my concern what you see right now. I'm only interested in what you saw last night."

"I'd like a nurse, please."

"You'll get a nurse when I get the answers I want. First off, you were found as a trespasser. Who are you?"

"My name is Patrick Donovan. Father Patrick Donovan."

"A priest? Wow, that's a new one. OK, Father, what were you doing at the Leighton Mansion last night?"

"I...I don't recall any mansion."

"Listen, this isn't a congressional hearing, so 'I don't recall' isn't going to cut it."

"Who are you?"

"I'm police Detective Eisen."

"Am I in trouble?"

"You tell me."

"I don't remember anything."

"You were found face down on the grass outside the premises of an historic mansion. You were unconscious. What were you doing there?"

"I told you, I don't'..."

"Yeah, yeah, yeah, you don't know," Eisen interrupted. "Tell me this, what is a priest doing out and about that late at night?"

"Maybe I was doing God's work."

"That late, huh? Wow, God must have a lot of work to do to have you humping it overtime."

"Am I under arrest?"

"Is there a reason that I should arrest you?"

"I told you, I don't know anything. I can't remember anything."

"Last chance."

"I'd like a nurse in here. Is there a doctor?"

"OK, we'll play your way," she said as she pulled out a pair of handcuffs and slapped one end quickly around Donovan's wrist and the other to the bed rail

"Hey, wait!"

"I'll go get your nurse, give you some time to recollect your thoughts. Then I'll be right back to read you your rights."

"Nothing?"

Eisen leaned back against the wall outside the patient room. She shook her head in disbelief at the news her partner was giving her. She did manage a weak smile for the doctor and nurse going in to attend to the young priest.

"Not a thing," Erikson replied. "The entire estate was clean. I mean, the cleaning crews that go through there keep it tidy, but I'm talking about no trace of anyone other than the caretaker. No forced entry, no prints, no hair, no fibers, I'm talking nada. The tech boys only did a precursory sweep because I asked them to, but not a thing, no."

Eisen turned her attention back through the observation window to Father Donovan. The doctor was checking his eyes with a light as the nurse took notes.

"Who found him?"

"The caretaker."

"They have a caretaker? Nice."

"Yeah, he was doing his rounds, same routine every day. Said he noticed what he thought was a man stumbling around in the courtyard. When he went to investigate, the man was prone and unresponsive. He called 911 and here we are."

"And this caretaker, he didn't hear any alarms?"

"He was in his quarters all night, said he didn't notice anything."

"Didn't notice any alarm?"

"He didn't hear one. They're silent alarms, but they're wired to give signal in the caretakers and servants quarters." Erikson starred down at the remnants of his coffee, swirling the cup so that the grounds became evident. "Hey," he said pointing in at Donovan, "this guy is really a priest, huh?"

"He was found with a celebret in his possession. It could be a fake, though; the name was inked out."

"Celebret?"

"Some sort of papal ID. It more or less gives them permission to perform mass outside their diocese. It proves they're a priest."

"Hmmm," said Erikson as he swallowed the last bit of coffee, grounds and all.

"Anything missing," she asked.

"Not at thing."

"The Davenport's had a safe; that was the target. Similar cases, same thing. The Leighton's must have had a safe."

"Yeah, but it wasn't opened."

"How can you tell?"

"The caretaker said it had a separate alarm. It never went off."

"I'd like to get it opened, check the contents, just in case."

111

"Are we going to get a warrant for that?"

"No, just a courtesy call to this Leighton fellow so he can make sure everything is there."

"The caretaker said that if anything happens in that house, he calls the estate manager."

"Where's he?"

"Vacationing in the South of France. And Leighton, according to the caretaker, is on safari in Africa or some exotic place hunting big game."

She turned her attention again to the doctor as he finished examining the priest. He then nodded to her, said something to the priest, closed his chart and walked towards her. He nodded again as he closed the door behind him.

"He appears to be fine," the doctor reported.

"Any reason he was found unconscious," Erikson asked.

"No, none that we could determine. We did a precautionary CAT scan when he was brought in. Everything was negative; no signs of a concussions or other trauma to the brain."

"He complained that he can't see," Eisen added.

"Yes, I checked. He responds normally, pupil dilation and contraction and all. It was most likely caused by some kind of sensory trauma. I'm certain his vision will return in a few days. On top of that, he doesn't seem to remember much, though he knows his identity, which is a good sign.

"How long can you keep him?"

"You handcuffed him to the bed. I'm assuming you want him to stay. Is he under arrest?"

"He could be."

"Well, let me know. I'd like to keep him under observation for a few days anyway. We have an electronic device we can use to keep track of him. We use it on

112

dementia patients so we know if they leave their room and wander off. Truly state of the art monitoring."

"The cuffs aren't good enough?"

"Detective," the doctor began in a hushed tone, "this is private hospital. We like to exercise a certain amount of discretion here. We have patients, wealthy patients as you can guess, that come here for, let's just say, some R and R. We'd prefer to use our own methods of restraint. Handcuffs will cause, well, some distraction. If you wanted to jail him, you should have requested him be sent to the county hospital."

"Why wasn't he sent to county," Erikson asked.

"The caretaker requested he be taken here."

"And why is that?" Eisen demanded.

"I make good money, better than most doctors, but our patients, I couldn't even begin to imagine the kind of money they have. If someone is injured on their property, they'd most likely take care of everything. Keep it out of the papers, you see, limit their liability."

"Well," Erikson added, "on my next bender, I'll make sure to pass out in this neighborhood. Get a free ride to a nice place like this."

"Oh yeah," the doctor added dryly, "that's if the dogs guarding most of the estates don't find you first. Now, I have other patients to attend to, so if you'll excuse me."

Chapter 18

The detectives left the hospital in silence. Eisen lit up a cigarette as they walked to their car in the ER lot. She exhaled shapeless forms of gray that mimicked the sky above. The sun was setting now, or had to be, but it was impossible to tell through the thick cloud cover. She thought it might rain again and pulled at the neck of her coat to ward off the chill.

They drove along in silence. She cracked her window and lit another cigarette and although Erikson shot her a look, he said nothing. He merely opened his window more and feigned a cough, but she was elsewhere, lost in thoughts, in conversations with ghosts he didn't wish to give life to.

"Hey," she said at last, flicking the butt of her smoke out the window and powering it up, "you ever have a dog?"

"When I was a kid, yeah; a poodle," he said as he rolled his eyes at her. "It wasn't my choice, it was a gift. I hated that dog."

"No, I was just thinking about something the doctor said."

"About where I'd end my bender?"

"Yeah, something about guard dogs."

"What about 'em?"

"There were none at the mansion."

"Yeah, they don't need them, everything there is electronic."

"Electronics can be beaten, gotten around."

"So can a dog. They can be drugged, shot, preoccupied."

"How do you preoccupy a dog?"

"Old trick I learned from my grandfather; ground hamburger, never more than rare done, pushed into a ball of peanut butter. The roof of a dog's mouth has ridges and the peanut butter sticks there. They can't bark and won't bite anything if they have something in their mouth. That's the humane way to take them out of the equation."

"And you learned this from your grandfather?"

"Long story. OK, so what about the dogs?"

"I just thought that if they don't have dogs, they must have one hell of an alarm system. Something state of the art, maybe."

"I guess I didn't see it."

"Cameras?"

"One would guess."

"Can we swing by and check out those cameras?"

115

"You know, we really should call it a day, Deb. We should check in, see what's what, you know, before the captain is on our ass."

"It's on the way…"

The caretaker escorted them through the large entry into an even larger grand hall. Eisen craned her neck to take in the frescoes that clung to the vault high above. The caretaker seemed to read her thoughts, or more precisely, he knew she was thinking what everyone unaccustomed to such surroundings thought.

"It's three stories."

"Why such a large room? You could almost play football in here."

"The master used to host such grand events with hundreds in attendance."

"Master, huh," she chided, "is that what he likes to be called?"

"It is only proper, Miss."

"I like your accent."

"Thank you, Miss."

"Is it English?"

"Welsh."

"Is there a difference?"

"A considerable one, Miss."

He led them out of the hall through a large alcove and into the servant's pantry that ran alongside the kitchen. They exited into a service corridor and walked down one flight of stairs to another service corridor, which eventually led them to the security room.

The caretaker pulled a card from his pocket and pressed it against a black panel next to the door lever. A light on the panel turned green and the lock made an audible click, signaling it was now open. He turned the lever and

116

pulled the door open and extended a hand for Eisen to enter. He then added an exaggerated bow as if mocking her, but she ignored this. He followed them into the room, leaving the door to automatically close and lock securely behind them.

"As you can see," he began as he typed furiously at the keyboard, bringing a bank of screens to life, "nothing was recorded."

"What causes the cameras to record?"

"Movement, light, heat; and sound when it's working properly."

"It was stormy last night," Erikson countered, "wouldn't the trees be swaying and make the cameras activate?"

"Oh no, these are very complex cameras. They have thermal sensors, very sensitive, they activate if they pick up a heat signature, body heat, but they discriminate between the heat signature of an animal and a human."

"So, if this guy that you found on the lawn last night wanders onto the property, where's the footage of that?"

"I'm afraid nothing was recorded."

"So, it malfunctioned," Erikson stated.

"Oh, no, this system has its own diagnostics. It essentially cannot malfunction."

"So this guy just shows up out of nowhere?"

"Well," the caretaker began, "there's this that I found odd."

He typed again at the keyboard and the screens went completely white, every monitor a blinding bright absence of anything.

"So it did malfunction," Eisen added.

"No, Miss, if you look at the data log, the light meter is off the charts. It's as if the cameras were all looking at the sun.

"They went blind," Erikson said as he shot Eisen a look. She nodded and smiled.

"Yes, I suppose you could say that," the caretaker mused, "but their angles of adjustment, their inclinations never changed."

"OK," Erikson said, "I think we've seen everything we need."

"Or not," joked Eisen.

"Yes," Erikson laughed, "or not. Thank you for your time."

"Certainly sir, anything to be of assistance. Allow me to show you out."

"Oh, we can manage," Erikson responded.

"I'm afraid that's quite out of the question; house rules and all."

As the massive doors to the mansion closed behind them, Eisen paused on the landing taking in the grounds.

"This is actually kinda nice."

"You mentioned that while we waited for the caretaker. I thought you weren't impressed," Erikson said as he descended the large steps.

"Yeah but this, this is really cool. I've only seen this place in magazines, but it's amazing up close."

Erikson stopped after the last step and bent down and slid his hand across the large stone slab, then along the edge where it abutted against the grass. He then stood up and surveyed the courtyard, beautiful bright green grass, trimmed neatly, off-set by large stone slabs arrainged in an alternating pattern, radiating outward from a large central fountain, the pattern mimicking the geometry of a dart board.

"I think it's marble. I wonder if they ever worry about cars dripping oil."

"I think," Eisen stated, "that if you have this kind of money, your cars don't drip oil."

"Ain't that the truth," he added almost absentminded, still looking about the grounds, taking in their beauty as if this were the last time he'd see such magnificence.

"Shall we then?"

"I'm all set," Erikson said.

"Back to the hospital," she intoned sweetly.

"No. We need to check in."

"We can call in."

"Deb, look, don't get mad."

"About what?"

"I'm supposed to personally make sure you check in after every shift."

"Oh, so you're responsible for me now?"

"No, look, it's not that. It wasn't my idea. I didn't want to do it, but it was either this or they pull you off onto a desk."

"How very generous of you!"

"Don't put this on me."

"I should thank you?"

"Look, you're not making this easy, not on yourself and certainly not on me. I'm the only reason you're out here, the only reason you're still on the case. I saw your shrink, did you know that? As your partner, they called me in and asked me about all kinds of shit. I lied to them Deb, lied to them, told them whatever I thought would make them keep you active, because I know you don't belong behind that desk. But you've got to meet me halfway. You need to start opening up to the psychiatrist, tell him something, anything. Just get him to know what I know and that is that you're not completely fucked up over this. But it doesn't matter what I think. It matters what they think."

"And what do you think?"

"Deb, com'on."

"No, what do you think? Tell me. I'm supposedly this big girl, all grown up and responsible, so tell me."

"Thousands of people have lost children," he began, then paused as he saw the daggers in her eyes. He waited a minute more for a verbal torrent to be unleashed, but she instead looked away, pulled out a cigarette and lit it with trembling hands.

"Deb, what I mean is, let this fuel you, let this drive you, but don't let this destroy you."

She looked back at him, tears welling up in her eyes, but her stubbornness refused to let them flow. She sniffed, drew heavily on the cigarette in an attempt to steady herself and exhaled loudly and forcefully, signaling in her own small way that she had surrendered, but also that the conversation was over.

"Deb, I'm sorry," he said.

"Can we please go to the hospital, pretty please? With sugar on top?"

"That sultry voice of yours will get you nowhere with me."

"No?"

He knew it could, and it did, but he held his ground despite the advantage that she held over him.

"I'm just saying," he said.

"So, we can go?"

"A quick in and out."

"I like that," she joked.

"If he's asleep, we go," he said, ignoring her comment. "If he's awake, five minutes max. Understood?"

She nodded as she exhaled once more, then dropped the cigarette onto the stone slab and ground it out with the sole of her shoe.

"Ah, don't do that," Erikson scolded.

"Sorry," she said, moving her sole over it to wipe away the black mark, now an indelible part of the stone.

"I guess you're right," Erikson said, "it is marble."

Chapter 19

Donovan tensed as he thought he heard the door to his room open, but he didn't hear it close and he heard no footsteps. He relaxed a bit, felt the edge of the bed rail against his elbow, felt the wrist band, heavy with the attached device strike the edge of the rail as he sat up.

He was startled when a hand suddenly put pressure upon his shoulder. He inhaled sharply and was about to call out when another hand landed firmly on his mouth, denying any attempt to call for help.

"Shhhh," he heard near his left ear. "I'm a friend; I'm here to help you. You're not going to scream, right?"

Donovan nodded up and down, the hand on his mouth following suit. He felt the hand leave his face. He inhaled deeply again, but kept quiet. The hand on his shoulder disappeared as well, only to reappear with the other hand on his right wrist, where the heavy, cumbersome object was attached.

"These things are tricky," he heard the voice say. "They're wired to activate a tracking device and alarm if they're not removed with the proper tool."

"Who are you?"

"You don't recognize my voice?" he heard the man reply, sounding almost wounded.

"No."

"Don't worry, you'll remember, give it time."

"Great," Donovan answered sarcastically.

"Ok," the man said as Donovan felt the device tighten painfully around his wrist. "Dammit! It shouldn't have done that."

"Done what? What happened?" Donovan asked as he tried to pull his hand away.

"Nothing to get excited about. Just stay calm, and stay still. I can't work with you moving your arm."

"Sorry," Donovan replied.

"He should've sent Crispis or Slava for this," the man mumbled to himself.

"Who?"

"Boy, you really don't remember, do you?"

"Slava, Slava," Donovan repeated, "that's a nice name."

"Oh, you definitely lost your memory," the voice said, laughing.

Donovan felt the man's hands pulling at the device until it began to vibrate intermittently.

"Why is it vibrating?"

"Oh, it's doing that too, huh?"

"What do you mean 'too'?"

"Well, it's flashing."

123

"Flashing? Is that bad?"

"Well, it sure ain't good. You want the good news or the bad news?"

"Bad news."

"If I monkey any more with it, it might go off. And I don't think I can remove it."

"And the good news?"

"I don't think I have to. Just hold still. This is probably going to hurt like crazy.

"What is? Wait!"

Before Donovan could protest he felt a powerful jolt rocket up his arm, into his chest and extend throughout his entire body. He felt his jaw clamp down, felt his teeth press together violently and he felt the tremors begin. He felt like he going to pass out, but almost as soon as the sensation started, it stopped. He lay there, breathing rapidly; unable to move, barely cognizant of what was going on around him.

Donovan heard muffled noise, slowly realizing that the sounds were speech. He began to feel the impact of a hand slapping at his cheek. He felt as if he were being rudely awakened after a deep sleep. He finally could make out the sounds and the voice of the man trying to revive him.

"Com'on, now," Donovan heard the voice say as he finally recognized it's owner.

"Mac?"

"Bingo! Welcome back. Now work with me Donovan, I got to get you into this wheelchair. We don't have much time before this tracking device resets itself."

"What, what did you do? I feel dizzy."

"Yeah," Mac said as he hoisted Donovan over his shoulder and swung him around into the wheelchair set up next to the bed, "I had to give it a shock and since it was attached to you, you got it too."

"How kind of you," Donovan said, trying to laugh despite the tingling sensation that caused him to wince.

"Always thinking of my fellow man," said with a smile.

Once settled in the chair, Mac wheeled him into the hallway. It was late, so the staff was a skeleton crew, mostly there to keep a watchful eye until morning. He turned towards the elevators and was fifteen feet away when he almost ran right into an attending nurse that had just left a patient's room. He brought the chair to a stop and smiled at the nurse, craning to read her name tag.

"Why, good evening Nurse Abbott. How are you this fine evening?"

"I am fine, thank you. And why are you taking this patient out of his room," she said as she looked at her chart, "I see no order for him to be about."

"No miss, of course not, the doc ordered an MRI..."

"Not another one," she interrupted.

"Yeah," Mac added, trying not to sound unaware, "something he wanted to check, I guess."

"Do you have the order?"

"Sure, I have it right here," he said as he feigned to look through his pockets. "Oh, no, I think I left it downstairs."

"I need that order."

"Shucks, miss, it's my first day and I'm trying to make a good impression. I really don't want to get in trouble over this. Can I bring it back on my return trip?"

"Hmm," she said as she eyed him suspiciously. "Well, seeing as you have the alarm bracelet turned off, they must have given you the code, so I believe you. Just make sure I have it when you return, or else we'll both be in trouble."

"Yes ma'am," he said as he wheeled past her to the elevator bank and pressed the down button. He looked back to find her staring at him, but she finally smiled and went back to her business of checking her rounds. He watched her disappear into another room and when the elevator doors opened, he backed the wheelchair into the cab quickly.

"Phew, that was close," Mac exhaled as the elevator doors closed after him.

The ride to the main floor went without interruption. When the doors opened, Mac popped his head out and looked down the long corridor. No one was in sight. He only had to worry about getting past the main desk, but he had that figured out. He pulled the wheelchair into the hall and pushed it towards the entrance.

He got maybe twelve steps when the sliding doors at the entrance slid open to allow a man and a woman to enter. They walked quickly to the desk. Mac, slowed his pace to a crawl. He then saw the man pull out a wallet and flash a police badge.

"Damn!"

"What?"

"Shhhhh. Quiet now," he warned Donovan as he spun the wheelchair around and headed back the other way.

"What?" Donovan repeated.

"Cops."

"Cops? Like those ones from earlier?"

"Apparently so. Shit and I'm parked out front. Damn, this really messes with my getaway. I'll never hear the end of this from Crispis if his ride gets pinched. I had this all planned out. Got my ID badge all tight and everything. Damned if something always goes wrong."

"So how are we getting out of here?"

"Through the morgue."

"What? No, no way," Donovan said.

126

"They have a loading dock. That's the only other means of egress that won't cause suspicion."

"You're gonna wheel me out of the morgue?"

"Gurney is more like it."

"What?"

"I have to lay you down on a gurney and cover you up. Play like I'm taking you to a funeral home. Don't worry; they usually retrieve the bodies at night. Nobody wants to see that shit during the day. It'll be all right."

Mac pushed Donovan up to the secure door at the end of the hallway. He placed his badge against the wall and held his breath as the doors finally began to swing open for him. When he turned around, he found the detectives waiting at the elevator, both of them watching him. He kept himself between Donovan and the detectives and offered a smile and a nod of the head. They stood resolute, offering no expression in return. With the doors open now, he wheeled Donovan through the opening and as the doors closed behind him, he heard the elevator ding its arrival. He waited a moment, and then snuck a peak through the glass vision panel on the door. He watched as the two detectives entered the cab and was relieved to see the doors finally slide closed behind them.

Chapter 20

"What do you mean 'gone'?! How can he be 'gone'?!"

Eisen slammed her hand on the nurse's desk, the echo from the impact repeating itself down the corridor.

"Please, Miss," Nurse Abbott implored, "please keep your voice down."

"You need," said Eisen as she caught the tone and volume of her voice, "you need to find him. He was not supposed to leave this room."

"We cannot hold him prisoner."

"He was supposed to be in police custody, but the doctor refused and suggested we accept your methods of keeping a patient from leaving."

"I can appreciate that Detective Erikson, but I have no control over those decisions."

"But you do have control of what happens on your floor, do you not?"

"Yes."

"You are head nurse, right?"

"Yes I am, but…"

"Then how can he just disappear?"

"I am trying to determine that!"

"Then why not pick up the phone and call the head doctor, or the hospital administrator and we can all sit down and figure this thing out?"

The nurse gave Eisen a stern look, but her eye contact wavered and after a moment, she looked away.

"You fucked up, didn't you?" Eisen said curtly.

"Please…"

The nurse fingered her metal shift chart nervously, and let it fall to the desktop. She followed suit and fell heavily into her chair.

"How long have you worked here?"

"Eighteen years," she said without looking up.

"Wow, that's a lot. I mean, you're probably close to retirement."

"Yes."

"Full pension?"

The nurse nodded.

"That would be awful to lose that now."

"Please don't."

"I mean, you might get a reprimand, but something tells me that if this gets out, all those rich people who rely on your discretion, what are they gonna do? Are they gonna continue to give all those donations, pay all those outrageous expenses, attend your fundraisers? I doubt it. And the publicity? I mean, when I report this, its public record."

"What do you want?"

"Do you still have his effects?"

"I believe so, yes."

"Get them."

"And the tracking code for the restraint," Erikson added.

"I'm not sure what that is," the nurse replied.

Erikson pulled out a knife and stepped toward the nurse. She backed away in horror.

"I told you, I don't know what..."

"Move," Erikson said.

She stepped aside as the detective walked past and stopped at a locked cabinet. He pushed the knife into the lock and twisted until the latch broke. He opened the door, and pried the metallic tag off the only wristband charger that was empty.

"The people who took the priest did this. Do you understand?"

The nurse shook nodded yes.

"Good. Now run along and get the things Detective Eisen requested."

Eisen paused as they exited the hospital and reached her hand into the large bag the nurse had given her. She fished around until she found what she was after; the celebret. She pulled it out, then closed the bag and stuffed it into the nearest trash bin. She then opened the folded piece of paper and began to read it as they walked to the car.

"You couldn't find a collection box for the clothes?" Erikson asked.

"Do you see one around here? Maybe someplace to donate a used Bentley?"

"Ok, ok," he relented, "now what?"

"First we check in."

130

The look of surprise on Erikson's face gave him away before he could open his mouth.

"Yes, you heard me. Then we go home, get a good night's sleep and first thing in the morning we go to the rectory listed on this most hallowed piece of paper, find the priest, figure out what's what and go from there."

Chapter 21

"St. Sebastian, huh?" Erikson remarked, looking up through the car windshield at the towering steeple of the church.

"Yep," replied Eisen, "that's what it says, St. Sebastian's Cathedral."

"That's an awfully big church for such a young priest. You sure he's the right guy?"

"You were expecting something smaller?"

Erikson got out of the car to get a better view.

"Yeah, much smaller."

"Well, this part of town isn't the greatest."

"That means that at one time," Erikson said, "this was a good part of town and maybe that could have something to do with his having such a large church."

"Well, if this is correct, it's his church. Let's go see his holiness."

Erikson walked ahead of Eisen, who stopped and watched as he ascended the stone steps to the large pair of wooden doors supported and held together by elegantly wrought iron work. He pulled at the handle, but the doors would not budge. He looked for a bell of some sort and when he found none, he began to pound on the door with his fist. The only sound he heard was the snickering coming from behind him. He turned to see Eisen, leaning against the car door, trying very hard not to laugh.

"Something funny?"

"When's the last time you went to church?"

"Long time ago. Why?"

"They lock the church."

"They lock it?"

"When mass is not in session, yes. Churches get broken into too, ya know."

"So, what now?"

"We go around back to the rectory, which is where the priest lives. He should be there."

They walked to the end of the block, and then turned up the next street adjacent to the church. Erikson commented on the size, on how dirty the exterior was, on how extraordinary it must have looked in its day. Eisen ran her fingers along the wrought iron fence that ran along the edge of the sidewalk as she walked. They passed the rear of the church, crossed the parking lot and headed for the much smaller building constructed of similar materials at the rear of the property.

They found the rectory door unlocked. They entered and quickly found the secretary's office. She was busy speaking with a young woman. Eisen took note that she was maybe five foot eight, slender, with long ravenous hair and

133

piercing blue eyes. While they couldn't make out the conversation, they noticed the young woman become increasingly frustrated and emotional. The conversation ended abruptly and as the woman left, she accidentally bumped into Erikson. As the woman apologized, Detective Eisen noticed that she was crying. She watched as the woman ran off to the bathroom just down the hall. When she turned back, she herself nearly ran into the secretary, who was now standing at the door to her office.

"May I help you?" the secretary inquired.

"I'm detective Eisen and this is my partner Detective Erikson. We're looking for Father Donovan. Is he available?"

"Well, he certainly is becoming quite popular today. However, I must apologize, he isn't here."

"Could you give us his whereabouts," Erikson asked.

"Is he in some kind of trouble?"

"Why do you ask?"

"Well, you're police detectives and I imagine you're here to question him about something."

"That's correct, ma'am."

"Twenty-five years as a paralegal," she gushed, "and now I do this in my retirement."

"It's obvious you haven't lost your touch," Erikson added admiringly, "but no, he's not in trouble. We just need to speak with him."

"Well, I'd love to help," she said, "but he's on sabbatical."

"Sabbatical," Erikson repeated.

"Oh yes, off doing God's work."

"Where?" Eisen asked.

"Why, I believe it was Africa; exactly where I'm not sure. I know he intended to start in Zambia, but he wanted

134

to keep his travel plans open, you know, go where the spirit of the Lord compels him."

"Does it compel him to stay here?"

"No, I said Africa. You know, elephants, savannahs, home of Tarzan."

Eisen pulled out the Celebret, opened it and handed it to the secretary. She took it and as she looked at it, a puzzled look came across her face.

"What is this?" the secretary wondered aloud.

"It's a celebret."

"I know what a celebret is. What are you doing with it? Father Donovan wouldn't need one when on a mission. And besides, I'd have known of this, since I'd be the one who types up requests for things like that. Where did you find it?"

"He apparently lost it," was Eisen's response.

"Hmmm, well then it must be a forgery," she said trying not to sound wounded but failing at her task.

"Why forge a document such as this?"

"If he had needed it, he would have asked me to procure one from the Cardinal. I would have known about it. I know about everything he does, I'm his secretary."

"Everybody has sides that we'd just as soon not show anybody. Secret sides, if you will," Eisen intoned.

"Not Father Donovan. He is a man of God," she said defensively. "There is obviously a mistake. He is in Africa on sabbatical doing God's work. Now, is there anything else I can help you with?"

"We'd like to see his room."

"Up the stairs."

"Don't you need to show us?" Eisen asked.

"We don't lock our interior doors, not even to the rooms the priests occupy. We have nothing to hide."

Eisen removed the Celebret from the woman's fingertips; the shock of this small betrayal still lingered on the old woman's face. Eisen offered her a terse smile and walked back into the hallway. Erikson offered the woman his card and told her to call him if the priest checks in. She nodded, accepted the card and disappeared into her office, closing the door behind her.

"Now that's a woman scorned," Erikson whispered as they ascended the staircase.

"What do you mean?" Eisen asked.

"I mean professionally. You can tell she takes great pride in her job, takes it very seriously. You almost get the feeling that she'd lie for him."

"She's a terrible liar."

"No, no, she wasn't lying, she was genuinely hurt! She knew the Celebret was legit. She's in there right now trying to figure out why he'd exclude her assistance in the matter."

"Good for her, let her stew."

They approached the priest's room and indeed found it had no lock. They opened the door and stepped inside. The room appeared neat. Eisen walked around the bed and pulled the duvet down and leaned in close to the pillow. Here, she found a single strand of hair and held it up so Erikson could see.

"He's been here," he said.

"But he won't be back. He knows we'd know where to find him."

"He's got to be staying somewhere local."

"Now that the trails gone cold, it's going to be tough to find this guy," Eisen said.

"We've got his tracking device, remember? The doctor said they could track their patients with it."

"I'm sure he's gotten that thing off by now. And besides, the range on that was maybe a mile or two from the hospital."

"Maybe, maybe not," Erikson said as he punched numbers on his cell.

"And there is no way we're going to be able to get a warrant to gain access to their tracking system, not in this short amount of time."

"Damn," Erickson said, shaking is cell. "I need to find a better signal. Let's head downstairs."

They left the room and headed back downstairs, Erikson walking quickly and a few steps ahead of his partner.

"Maybe we won't need a warrant," he said over his shoulder.

"What do you mean?"

"Give me a minute," he said, holding the phone to his ear, "it may be nothing and it may be everything."

"I'll take anything at this point."

Erikson's voice trailed off as he turned away from his partner and spoke in hushed tones to an anonymous voice on his cell.

"Excuse me."

Eisen turned around to find the woman who'd been in the office before them. She held her composure now, but Eisen could tell her eyes were puffy and red from crying.

"Can I help you?" Eisen offered.

"Well, forgive me, I don't wish to seem nosy, but you're detectives, right?"

"Yes."

"Well, I saw you talking to Father Donovan's secretary on my way out and I overheard your conversation. I wasn't eavesdropping, really, I just…it seems like we're after the same thing."

Eisen looked at her partner, now busy with a private conversation on his cell. She looked again at this woman and thought maybe this will offer something to go on. Half of nothing is better than all of nothing.

"My name is Patricia," the woman said, extending her hand. "There's a coffee shop a block over. It's rarely busy, so it's a good place to talk. I mean, it's busy after mass, but on weekdays it's kinda dead."

"Perfect," Eisen replied.

Chapter 22

"How are you feeling?"

Donovan heard the voice as if it were receding into the distance. Despite his blindness, he looked in the direction of the voice and nodded.

"Who's there?"

"It's Judas."

"Judas, I, I'm sorry, I screwed things up."

"On the contrary, it is I who seek your forgiveness. I know we haven't spoken much since you've joined us. I'm either asleep or doing what I do, which causes me to sleep even more, I'm afraid. I've been a terrible host."

"No, I understand."

"No, you don't. I truly appreciate your kindness, but no one could possibly understand."

"But you rescued me," Donovan protested.

"No, Mac rescued you."

"But I thought Slava or Crispis…"

"Mac is more than my caretaker. He is very capable. He has been with me the longest, and knows me as well as I know myself."

"How long has he been with you?"

"Almost seven hundred years."

"He's that old?"

"Physically, no. He ages differently, as do Slava and Crispis. However, his soul is that old, if not older. When I met him, I could sense his wisdom. There are a great many things you can learn from a man like Mac."

"He's so unassuming."

"The greatest among us often are."

"How did you meet?" Donovan asked eagerly.

"I can assure you, our meeting was not nearly as notable as the others. He was charged with the task of bringing the dead to burial, as were many of his kind, during the great plague. The job essentially came with a death sentence, but he went about his task with great compassion. He would be sent into the homes to retrieve the bodies. Imagine, if you can, how heart wrenching it is to remove a body, maybe the father, from a family that is grieving, yet they cannot properly say good-bye for fear of infection. And inevitably, he'd return to the same house and remove the wife, perhaps, or the child."

"Eventually, he becomes infected himself," Judas continued. "He still carries on his task, despite the failings of his body. He takes the last corpse of the evening to the burial site, places it in the trench, then collapses and falls in himself. He's lying there with all the other corpses, staring at the night sky, waiting for his turn to come. He's at peace."

"Why did you save him, then?" Donovan asked.

"I pulled him from the mass grave and before I could utter a word, he bids me to leave before I become infected with this curse."

"'What do you know of curses?' I ask him."

"'It is God's will.'"

"'You feel you have angered him or displeased him? Is this how you justify such misery?'"

"Delirious now, he confesses, mistaking me somehow for, well, who knows what. I am so moved by his words, so touched as I had not been for many years."

Donovan heard a scrapping sound, as if a chair were being dragged across a stone floor. The sound stops just in front of him.

"So I gave him a chance at redemption."

He could feel Judas' breath upon his face, and then he felt his palms on his eyes.

"How is your vision?"

"I can't see anything," Donovan replied.

"Can you see lights? Can you make out shadows?"

"Nothing. It's all darkness."

"Hmm," Judas grunted, then rubbed his hands together and placed his palms back on Donovan's eyes.

"Hold very still. Try not to move your head."

"What did Mac do, to warrant a second chance?"

"That is between him and his God, when his time comes. Now, please hold still."

Donovan felt warmth from his touch. He felt this warmth spread across his brain, much like a headache would in its attempt to takeover, but there was no pain, only bliss. He felt the warmth caress him, flow down his neck. He could feel it in his throat, in his chest. He felt lightheaded, he felt sleepy. He lost control of his composure and slumped forwards into Judas.

141

"Please, I need you to keep your head up."

Donovan tried to remain upright, but this sense of complete calm was taking over his body. He felt like he was at the threshold of sleep, but very alert. He felt his lungs filling up with air. He inhaled and noticed the sweet aroma of flowers. He thought he heard voices in the distance, but they were not voices, they were faint melodies; remnants of a mysterious code transcribed by delicate strings.

He tried to inhale this scent again, but couldn't. He found he was no longer breathing. His chest constricted; he felt pressure on every inch of his body and his eyes began to burn. He felt his body tremble, and then convulse. He lost all sense of coordination and tumbled to the floor.

Then it stopped.

He opened his eyes and found he could see again.

"It hurts, doesn't it?" Judas said as he helped Donovan to a chair, "I know. Not to be a martyr or anything, no pun intended, but what I experience is far worse."

"You didn't pass out," Donovan said.

"Yes, this type of blindness is special."

"Special?"

"You don't remember?"

"What is it that I am supposed to remember?"

"You saw God."

Donovan looked at Judas incredulously.

"You think it impossible?"

"Yes. No one can look upon the face of God."

"No mortal can look upon it. I am immortal. The others to a much lesser extent; they are still heir to all the elements that demise the body, but since I have saved them, they suffer them at a much lesser extent. But you are mortal, and thus the blindness. Imagine if you will, looking into the sun; not a good idea, but you get the gist. That is nothing compared to the brilliant aura surrounding God."

"Why don't I remember anything?"

"It's too much for the human brain to comprehend."

"So, God came to us."

"He came to me."

"What did he want?"

"My assistance."

"With what?"

Judas got up from the position in front of Donovan and crossed the room to a bar. He fixed two highball glasses with ice and filled them with a crystal liquid. He returned to offer the young priest a glass, which he accepted. He watched over the rim of his glass as Donovan took a sip.

"Do you like it?"

"It tastes like water."

"It is water, but unlike any that you could know. This water is very old. It is the way it should be; unspoiled."

"It's delicious."

"Do you know why I chose you?"

"The same reason you chose the others, I'd guess."

"No. I saved the others. They were dying. You were fine; physically anyway."

"Why then?"

"Actually," Judas laughed, "I was hoping you'd tell me. It's not every day I come across a priest about to jump from a bridge."

"I was merely contemplating it."

"You were lost."

"You can read minds, too?"

"No," said Judas with a hint of laughter, "but you were over the railing, so it wasn't difficult to figure out. I know the feeling though, believe me. How do you feel now? Better?"

143

"Much. Thank you."

"You're most welcome."

"So, your 'saving me' was accidental?"

"I didn't save you. Let's just say I kept you from a certain fate."

"What's the difference?" Donovan asked, looking down at the glass, now half full of the delicious water.

"Save, redemption, revive..."

"So, those you revive..."

"I prefer healing."

"OK, you heal people."

"I offer them a second chance. I offer them something that was never offered to me. I never thrust it upon them."

"It seems like a great gift."

"It's a curse. Do you know what it's like to watch those you love die in front of your eyes and there is nothing you can do about it?"

"I thought you could save people?"

"It didn't come with instructions. I didn't realize this power until sometime after it was bestowed upon me. I guess I should have known when I couldn't die by my own hand. I'm sure you're aware of that."

"In the bible it's told that you took your own life, but there are conflicting accounts."

"That I tried to stab myself and hang myself."

"Yes."

"I did both and neither successfully. That is why all mention of me stops there. Jesus dies, his body is not recovered and he is loved by all. I supposedly die, my body is never accounted for and I'm written off in history as a traitor. I paid greatly for my allegiance; I lost everything because I loved."

Judas emptied his glass and took Donovan's glass, still half full.

"Do you want more?"

"No thank you."

Judas shrugged and lifted Donovan's glass to his lips and consumed what remained.

"I tell you, it is easy to prepare for and accept death, even welcome it, but nothing will prepare you for the moment when you realize that you cannot die. I wanted to die, wanted it so badly, even though I knew that salvation would never be mine if I took my own life. What was the alternative? I 'betrayed' the son of God! I was going to hell any way you look at it. But to pursue death and be unable to achieve it? That is a curse and a punishment beyond any hell."

"What I didn't realize at first," Judas continued, "is that I had this 'gift.' I thought that perhaps God wanted to punish me in other ways, wanted to keep me alive to suffer the ever increasing guilt and anguish I felt, but wanted me to feel it in a much greater capacity. And he succeeded. I went away to distant lands, found a woman and was married. I had a semblance of a life, found a sliver of happiness, but the darkness was never far away."

"My wife was expecting our first child. I was off laboring, as I found physical labor exhausting and a welcome relief from my torment. I came home that night to find the midwife in tears. They were dying. I knew not what to do, so I sat and wept, afraid to touch either of them, certain that my existence in their life had brought this upon them. Can you imagine the rage I felt towards God long after I realized the power that I possessed?"

"I wandered for awhile after that. How long, I do not know. I wasn't aging, unbeknownst to me, so I had no idea of time passing, maybe a few hundred years? I arrived in a small village and found employment with a farmer. He was a kindly man, though poor and couldn't afford to pay me much. He did offer meager food and shelter in exchange for the most back breaking physical labor you can imagine, which I threw myself into. You would think that exchange insane, but I found it to be a blessing. I soon was beginning to forget about my wife and child. I would go a day without thinking about them, then two, then four, then a week and soon they were absent from my thoughts. But I could never banish from my mind what God had done to me. It was a dark time for me, and I grew very angry with God for having forsaken me."

"The man had a son, a small child. He had a daughter too, a few years older, and he loved her very much, but his son was his life. Back then, the son carried on everything. He was, in a sense, his immortality. The love this man had for his family, you could almost feel it, like heat given off by a fire. And while it did not warm me, being around it offered me my first sense of comfort in many, many years."

Judas returned to the bar and refilled his glass with water. He motioned to Donovan for more, but he declined. Judas drank the water quickly and filled the glass again before returning to sit by the young priest.

"I had not thought of my family for some time, and I was glad for this. Then, one day, while I was working deep in the fields, I think I was clearing rock from the ground. It was tough rock, and deep, stalling many efforts to cut an irrigation channel for new crops. I toiled many days before getting the desired depth so the water would flow."

"So, there I was, working, toiling really, it was getting dark and as I swung the last blow, I broke through and found soil. I fell back, exhausted, staring up at the darkening sky, happy for my small victory against God, for I was certain he placed those rocks to dishearten me."

"I lay against the bank, hearing only my breath when the young daughter's voice breaks over the hilltop."

"Joshua! Joshua! Come quickly, you are needed!"

"Who's Joshua?" Donovan interrupted.

"It was a name I took. I've gone by many names, many alias' through the years. I think you can appreciate how hard anonymity would be by introducing oneself as 'Judas.'

"Here she comes and I notice she is crying. She tells me the boy is dying. The family is distraught, so the father sends her to fetch me. This was quite an honor, since they considered me part of the family now. It was customary with this man that when one family member is dying, all family members should be by their side to wish them off. It's not uncommon, but to fetch me from the fields touched me and I ran off to join them."

"As I approached the boy, he looked at me and breathed his last breath. It was customary, for some reason, to hold the loved one in your arms when you said good-bye. I took him up in my arms and cradled him. I felt something wash over me, a feeling of uneasiness and pain, which I mistook for sadness. I became dizzy and passed out. When I woke, they were celebrating. The man was on his knees next to where I lay and he was kissing my face. He was crying; not for sadness, but for joy. They told me a miracle had happened; they told me that God had spared their son *through* me. I rose and tried to explain it away, but try making a believer not believe something. I did not take stock in it, disagreed with any who brought it up, until the next day."

"We were pulling the rocks from the ground. The day's work was much easier than in days past and hearts

147

were light and much joking and frivolity was at hand. One laborer, I forget his name, was not paying attention and slipped on the bank and fell. He landed in such a way that his throat fell against the one sharp rock in the pile. Blood began to spew forth. We all knew that he was as good as dead. One man ran off for help. I jumped into the ditch and place my hand on his throat; not in an effort to stop the bleeding, which I thought impossible, but to stem the flow so he couldn't see it and let him pass in relative peace."

"I talked to him of future events, anything to keep his mind off the fact he was dying; what tomorrow would bring, whom he would marry and how many children he'd have. The other man who left for help returned with the land owner and another man. As he approached, I rose from the injured man and climbed from the ditch. They froze, mouths wide open, the other laborer managing to point his finger just past me. I turned to see the dying man climbing up after me. His throat bore no mark, nor was there any blood. I looked at my hands and at my robe and they too were clean, not even the dirt from the day's labors was evident."

"'You have healed him, Joshua!' the land owner proclaimed. He hugged me, then the laborer whose life I saved. A big feast was planned for me that night. There was talk of inviting the holy men from the nearby village. As I cleaned up after the days labors, I overheard the land owner speak of his fortunes changing, that I would somehow heal the crops, bring him back to prosperity. His son, speaking from the purity of a child, told him I should heal others, fix other children. That set off a crazed look in the man. He began raving about bringing people far and wide to be healed. As I turned away, I heard him speak of how rich I was going to make him.

"I fled. I left my belongings, which weren't much. I ran over the fields where I once worked and kept going. I walked all night and most of the next day. I decided to avoid people; I changed my name again. I knew I could not stay in one place long."

"I felt cursed by God and now I felt his wrath more acutely; had I the power to save my own wife and child all this time? Where did this power come from and when did I attain it? Would it vanish just as mysteriously as it appeared?"

"And then it hit me. I remembered exactly how and when this 'gift' was bestowed upon me..."

Chapter 23

"They have great pies here, too," Patricia said as she stirred cream into her coffee.

Eisen watched the young woman fix her coffee as she waited for Erikson to return from the counter. The air indeed smelled wonderful from the aroma of bread being baked somewhere in the kitchen. She thought about getting up and ordering a warm croissant with butter, but remembered the reason why she was here.

Erikson arrived with their coffee. The young woman eased the cream and sugar across the table. The detectives smiled and shook their heads gently, as they both took theirs black.

"So," Eisen began, "how long ago did you meet Father Donovan?"

"A little over a year."

She sipped innocently at her coffee. Eisen watched her and though she wasn't the best at guessing age, she figured she couldn't be older than twenty-five.

"Yeah, that sounds right," she added. "And it was here in fact."

"What was the occasion?" Erikson asked.

"This place bakes bread for the church. You know those wafers they serve at communion at other churches? Well, St. Sebastian's served pieces of bread at communion. Oh, my goodness, it was so good! Baked maybe an hour before and still warm; they kept the loaves under a heavy cloth. When you went up to receive the body of Christ, the priest would tear off a piece of the bread. It was like maybe the way Jesus would do it way back then."

"Anyway," she continued, "after mass, everybody would meet here for coffee. It was nice, very quaint. The ladies of the congregation would sip their coffee at the tables and chit chat while the men tended to crowd around the counter near the kitchen. Armand, the baker, would play the football game on the radio in the back and the men would try and get within earshot without their wives catching on. Armand was a funny man, this little Italian, always singing, but goodness, you've never tasted bread like what came from his oven."

"And the priests would come to these little gatherings?" Eisen inquired.

"Oh yes. They would come and visit for a while with everyone. I guess it was a tradition started during the Great Depression. The bakery would serve food to everyone; not just the congregation, but anyone who'd come by. The priests would be here to see how the people were doing, see if they needed anything. After things got better, they kept it up, every Sunday after the noon mass."

"This is where you made his acquaintance?"

Eisen watched her nod her head as she brought the coffee to her lips. She put the cup back on the table and fidgeted with the handle, her gaze frozen on the cup.

Eisen gave Erikson a sideways glance. She saw he was watching the fingers of the young woman's right hand slide around the handle and skim across the lip while the fingers on her left tapped softly at the side.

Erikson turned to Eisen, who gave him a slight nod.

"You know what?" Erikson began, "Screw it. Excuse my language, but I'm going to get some pie. Ladies?"

"None for me," said Eisen.

"No thank you," Patricia said quietly, her eyes still on her coffee.

"How did you first meet him?"

"Here, after my first mass. I came in late, I had trouble finding the church and I was trying not to interrupt the sermon. I took my seat and afterwards things got very quiet. I found him staring at me. I thought, oh boy, great, but then he kept going with his sermon."

She lifted the coffee to her lips again, took a sip, and then began fidgeting again as soon as the cup was back on the table.

"I mean, I thought I was going to get a speech about interrupting a sermon when he introduced himself, but he didn't bring it up. He was very nice."

"Were the two of you close?"

Patricia froze, her lower lip trembled. She brought a hand to her head and pushed the hair off her face.

"Kind of, I mean, I guess."

Eisen noticed Erikson returning with his pie. She shot him a look that made him roll his eyes and head back to the counter.

152

"So, why were you looking for the priest today? You seemed anxious to find him."

"He was a friend."

"Close enough of a friend that it upset you? You were crying when you went off to the bathroom."

"You saw that, huh? Oh, how embarrassing!"

"It's ok. I take it he didn't tell you where he was going."

"No."

"You'd think he'd at least inform the congregation where he was going if he was leaving them."

"I wasn't part of the congregation at that time."

"You missed a few masses?"

"No, I left altogether."

"You left?"

"Yes."

"Any particular reason?"

"I didn't want to be a distraction."

"A distraction? In what way?"

"Look, I don't want to get him into any trouble, especially with the police..."

"We never said he was in trouble," Eisen interrupted. "We only wanted to ask him a few questions."

Patricia's lower lip tremble began to tremble. Tears were welling up in her eyes. She tried hard not to look at the detective, but when she finally made eye contact, she couldn't contain them any longer.

"I'm so sorry. I didn't mean for this to happen."

Eisen slid a comforting hand across the table and stroked the young woman's forearm.

"It's ok. It's ok."

"It's not. I ruined everything. I didn't mean to. It just, it just..."

Then Patricia lost all control. She began to weep heavily, and then she wailed at the top of her lungs. Eisen got up from her chair and knelt beside her, put her arms around her and held her, gently rocking her. She put one hand gingerly on the back of Patricia's head and with her fingertips, stroked her head with a light massaging motion.

"Shhhh," Eisen cooed.

Patricia buried her head against Eisen and let it all out. She cried like this for many minutes. Erikson watched at the bar as his partner consoled the young woman. He was concerned that meeting this woman would derail his plans. The appointment that he had gotten from his phone call at the rectory was not only hard to get, but one that wouldn't wait and he sensed that this wasn't going anywhere. Still, he afforded Eisen the chance to do her job.

He brought his cup of coffee to his lips but realized that he had already emptied it. When he looked to the man behind the counter, he saw he was riveted on what was happening between the two women. Erikson cleared his throat to get his attention and when that failed, he snapped his fingers. As if coming out of a trance the man came to attention and turned to Erikson. Erikson raised his cup and the man smiled and turned to retrieve the pot for a refill.

Eisen moved her head, positioning her mouth at Patricia's ear.

"Tell me what happened. I promise you it won't leave this room. He won't be in trouble for what you tell me."

She pulled herself back, sliding her arms down Patricia's shoulders, down her forearms, until she held the young woman's hands in hers.

"Tell me," Eisen said.

Patricia sniffed and took one hand back to remove the hair from her face and wipe her eyes. Then, in a gesture of trust, put her hand back in Eisen's grasp.

"We were lovers."

The look on Eisen's face didn't hold all the shock and surprise the woman expected, so she continued.

"It was innocent enough. It was just, from the first moment I saw him, I knew I loved him. I played it off as infatuation. I told myself I felt these feeling because he was unattainable. So, thinking I couldn't have him made it easier for me to connect with him. I never thought it would happen, never wanted it to happen, but then it did."

She sat upright again in her chair, freeing one hand from Eisen to sip at her cold coffee.

"And then he began questioning his calling."

"Questioning it how?"

"He told me he loved me, from the moment he laid eyes on me. He said it was a sign maybe that he should follow a different path."

"What kind of path?"

"I don't know. I couldn't understand him, really. He was touted as this biblical genius, you know, a true follower of Christ. The last thing I wanted was to be the one to blame for screwing all of that up."

"So you left."

"Yes."

"Do you think he ever tried to find you?"

"I don't know."

"Do you think his sabbatical had anything to do with you?"

"Maybe."

"I think it did," Eisen said. "I think maybe he went in search of his path, the one you started him on. Do you agree?"

Patricia nodded hesitantly.

"So you came back after how long?"

"Almost a year."

"And why did you come back?"

"I needed to talk to him."

"About what?"

"When I left, I was with child; his child."

Chapter 24

Judas rubbed the silver coins in his hand. The rough, uneven feel of their recent casting echoed the uneven thoughts in his head. This, he thought, this is the price of salvation?

He stared out at the sea, his eyes scanning the vast body of water before him. He could see that dawn was approaching; the slivers of light creeping over the horizon, already over the distant lands where he wished to be.

It is done, he thought, and about to be undone. Nothing can change the events he set in motion. He had met with the Romans last evening, laid out the plan as suggested to him. He found them surprisingly indifferent; the bounty given and off he was back into the streets as the last remnants of daylight faded.

He had a full jug of wine with him now, thinking he would get drunk. But drinking in sorrow is too close to drinking in happiness. The jug sat next to him, untouched all night.

He tried to think of something, anything to deter his mind from focusing on what was imminent. Happy times, though there were many, eluded him at this hour. His thoughts kept returning to what was done, what his part was and the sorrow that was upon him.

He sat on the shore all night, not sleeping, not feeling tired. He sat as if mesmerized by the waters ebb and flow, by the gentle tide. He sat thinking of the one man whom he had loved, the one person who was willing to sacrifice his life for him, but for what?

Judas disagreed with Jesus. He begged him to reconsider, and when Judas was asked of his part in this, he begged again. His friend was resolute.

"Please," he recalled saying, 'please make Peter do it. He is stronger. Look at him! He has the strength of many men."

"Your spirit is stronger," was Jesus' reply.

"Thomas? John? Anyone else, please."

"I must ask this of you, Judas."

"I cannot."

"Yes you can."

"I will not."

"Judas, look deep within your heart. Your love for me will allow this."

"It is my love that forbids it."

"There is no one else."

Judas could not come up with another name then, just as sitting here all night, he could not find another now. There was no one else. Certainly, many professed to love him, but who could have the will, the selflessness to do his bidding.

Then he thought back, remembered what he had said to him.

"I will do it. But not for them, not for the people you seek to save, not for the others and certainly not for me. I do this for you. If this is truly your desire, then I shall grant it, but only out of love."

"It is my wish."

"Then yes, Jesus, I will do so."

Jesus embraced him. Judas could feel the wiry muscles go taut in his thin body, could feel the pressure of each finger, of each hand, pressing his body into him. Judas held him just as tight, trying to teach his muscles the memory of this body, so he would always remember the physicality of this man that would be sacrificed and left to die.

Judas began to cry.

Jesus slid one hand slowly to the back of Judas' head and caressed him. He whispered something in his ear, something thinking back now that Judas did not want to remember.

"Do not weep for me," he added as he pulled away just enough so that they were now face to face.

"I cannot help it. I fear I may never see you again."

"Do you have no faith?"

"I have faith, dear Jesus, I do."

"Then you must trust me."

Jesus pulled away from his friend and smiled deeply at him.

"Come, we have a feast to attend, a last supper, if you will. We must not keep the others waiting."

The sun licked gently at the horizon, its rays lightening the day. The dawn was here and there was nothing Judas could do to stop it. Today is the day, he thought, today it all ends.

He got up from the cold sand on which he had sat all night, knocking the full vessel of wine over. The precious red liquid spilled forth, wasting itself upon the uncaring ground. Judas watched as the wine exhausted itself unto the earth. His blood will flow like this, Judas mused, it will spill just as freely and no one will care.

He kicked off his sandals and walked into the water. The coldness made him shiver, but it sharpened his senses. He looked down into his palm and saw the silver coins. There they had stayed all night, tightly bound in his grip until he could feel their presence no longer.

The rising sun caught the polished coins and they glistened in the early light. Though they looked brilliant, their newness was lost on him. Judas thought not of appearances, but of sums. This amount, he thought, this little for a man of such great importance? Judas was sure he could have demanded a much larger bounty, but what was the point? He did not want to be there in the first place. He was numb, out of himself, and he agreed to accept what they offered so it could be over and done with. He wanted his part in all of this to be over.

Except that it wasn't over. Not yet.

Jesus had one last request.

Judas was to lead the Romans to him. It could have been just as easy and more agreeable to Judas if he could just point Jesus out. They knew where to find him, after all, and they must have known Jesus would not flee. However, Jesus thought it most important that he find him alone in the garden.

160

"It is my wish that you are with me when you signal them," Jesus told him after their last meal together.

"I'd rather just stand in the shadows and point."

"No, you must come to me. Do you remember what I whispered to you earlier, when I took you in my arms and you cried? Do you not remember?"

"I do remember."

"Then it must be so. The signal must be a kiss."

Judas looked down into the cold waters that surrounded him now. He had waded, lost in thought, out into the water until he was waist deep. He felt at last a sense of peace, however slight. It is done, it will be done, it is out of my hands now, he thought. No, I can still stop it. But that is not his will. I will abide.

"It's time."

Judas heard his friend's voice behind him, but did not turn. He stood facing the rising sun, its light warming him. He held his eyes closed and slowly turned and began walking to the shore.

As he reached the shore, Jesus held his arms out to him, but he did not seek an embrace.

"Where are the others?" Judas asked.

"Asleep," Jesus replied, "well, drunk, really; passed out."

"Shall we then," Judas said, trying to hold his resolve.

"Shall we not have a drink first?"

"I have no wine."

"This will do," Jesus said, retrieving the empty wine jug. When he handed it to Judas, he felt its full weight. Judas smiled.

"That never gets old, does it?" Jesus asked.

"What shall we drink to then?" Judas inquired.

"Why don't we just share a drink? For fellowship."

161

They sat together on the sand and drank from the vessel and watched as the sun gained its full strength. Neither said another word to the other.

Judas did as he was asked. He walked across the garden and stood before Jesus as he prayed. Jesus rose and Judas caught something in Jesus' eyes he had not seen before. There was a glowing, as if light was radiating from inside him. Judas clasped his shoulders and upon touching him, felt strength, such a feeling of hope that was at odds with how he felt seconds ago.

Judas leaned forward and as was customary upon greeting a friend, kissed Jesus on the lips. He barely had time to pull back and look into his friend's eyes again before the soldiers descended, grabbing Jesus and forcing him to his knees. Judas was knocked backwards; his head reeling, his feeling of strength now disconnected from its source. He felt sick and light-headed as if he might faint. He was caught in the fray and while Jesus did not protest his arrest nor did he resist, the soldiers came prepared for violence nonetheless. Judas threw himself at the soldiers, trying to protect Jesus but was beaten down and rendered unconscious.

He woke hours later. It was Peter who roused him. He lifted Judas to his feet and shook him. He wanted to know where Jesus was.

"Gone," Judas replied.

"Gone? Gone where?"

"They took him."

"They?"

"Are you stupid, man?" Judas roared.

"The Romans," Peter surmised.

"Yes, the Romans. It was foretold."

"Who was it, Judas? Who betrayed him?"

"It was I."

162

Peter looked incredulously at Judas. He then raised a fist as if to strike Judas, but he did not move and Judas did not flinch. He saw no fear in Judas' eyes and this, for some reason, frightened Peter.

"Go from here! Go far away," Peter ordered, "for if I see you again I will surely murder you for sacrificing my Lord!"

"What do you know of sacrifice?"

Peter threw Judas to the ground and ran off. When he was gone, Judas collected himself and stood. The ground felt unstable and as he tried to take a step, he stumbled and fell. He lay there staring at the sky, at the fading light and knew his friend's earthly judgment was at hand.

"It's time."

He heard the voice again, but this time it was different. He saw the sky above quickly go black, and then slowly surrender to grey. He tried again to get up, and as he was rising from what he thought was still the garden, he saw the room slowly take shape. He was in his bedroom, far away from the garden and many, many years removed. He turned and saw Mac, holding the cold beverage that revives him.

"Wake up, Judas," said Mac. "It's time. They're waiting for your word."

Mac handed the glass to Judas and its coolness instantly made him think of the waters he had visited last night, the same waters he had visited on that night over two thousand years ago.

He drank from the glass and the liquid did rouse him. He got up from the bed and crossed over to the heavy curtains that kept the room dark. He pulled them apart and the sun exploded into the room.

"Sir, your eyes!"

"I am fine," Judas soothed, blinking rapidly in the blinding light. He was unable to see at first, but his eyes slowly became accustomed to the brightness.

"Mac?"

"Yes, I am here."

"Tell the others I have something for them to do today in preparedness for tonight. I want you to go as well."

"Are we planning to visit someone in particular this evening? I shall get everything ready."

"No, we are not going out. I feel that someone will call on us."

"I'll await your orders," Mac said as he left the room and closed the door.

Judas, now fully able to withstand the light, walked over to the window and looked out. He saw the refuse and decay that man's uncaring hand towards the world had wrought, but he was now thankful for it. He had taken refuge in an abandoned factory, miles from the city center, too close to toxic spills for there to be any neighbor, for anyone to be accidentally nosing around.

Yet he saw something in the city this morning. He saw it from a different perspective. Nothing had changed; his dream had only been a retelling of previous events. But something gave him pause, something brought forth a feeling he couldn't quite place.

It was part of the dream he was struggling to recall. Something that Jesus said, something forgotten all those years he was trying now to remember.

Then it hit him. How simple, indeed.

When Jesus consoled him and soothed his crying, he had whispered something in his ear. It was something so simple and so easily forgotten; words of solace often taken for granted in the efforts to elevate someone's spirits.

"Now Judas," he heard him whisper, "you will have a chance to find your soul or lose it forever."

He repeated these words aloud, felt them in his mouth, and heard them resonate in the air. He thought he once knew what Jesus meant, but he knew now he was wrong. He looked down at the dregs of his beverage and threw the glass violently against the wall.

Chapter 25

Patricia walked out of the café as dusk approached. She hadn't wanted to leave really; she would have preferred to drink one too many cups of coffee and be rendered sleepless. However, she sensed the interview with the police was over, like so many she encountered while job hunting; 'thank you for your time, now you may leave while we pass judgment over you.'

She pulled at her jacket, but didn't feel the need to zip it up. The air was still warm and while she didn't really need the jacket, she wanted to feel the pull of the leather comfort her, like an assuring arm slung tightly across her shoulders.

Patricia frequented that coffee shop everyday since she returned. She hoped she'd run into him, maybe on his way to the shelter, grabbing a quick cup of coffee or a latte and scone to start his day. She attended mass the past few Sundays and although he wasn't there, she'd still hope he would show afterwards for coffee with the elderly ladies, who'd bake some treats of their own and who'd sit with him and gossip for hours. He had a lovely nature like that, she recalled, making everyone feel important to him.

The past Sunday she sat at a two-top by the window, stirring more sugar than she'd enjoy into her coffee while waiting for him to show, hoping that this morning at last would produce him. The sun was brilliant and the day getting warm, so she thought today if any day, he would come.

She had let her third cup of coffee get cold as it became evident to her that today would not be the day. She placed her spoon neatly against a napkin and was about to get up when she noticed a slight coffee stain on the marble topped table. She hadn't noticed it when she sat down, but it triggered a memory. The young Priest's coffee cup had left that ring.

"I guess I can't drink a cup of coffee without dripping," he'd joked.

She rubbed at the remnant of the stain, deeply echoed into the marble. She remembered the first time he approached her, after her first mass. She sat in this same spot, starring out the window, lost in thought when she finally noticed the handsome young priest standing before her, offering her a warm smile.

"I said, 'is this seat taken?' "

"No, please."

After he sat he extended his hand and introduced himself.

"You're new to our Parish, or just stopping by?"

"I'm not sure."

167

"I only ask because, well, I remember every face that comes to mass. Names, a bit stickier, but I usually see the same faces every week and yours is new."

"Well, I just came into town last night, so I'm not too familiar with things."

"Well, some of the uptown churches are nicer, but we've got a great congregation here. They've got the newer churches, but we've got the striking Cathedral architecture. It truly is a blessing to share this with all the people."

"It's nice."

"So, where are you from?"

"Um, I need to get going."

She remembered how nervous she suddenly became talking to him. She could barely keep eye contact. There was something arresting about his gaze, something even familiar. Or was it something she'd simply never seen in a man before? Whatever it was, it made her self-conscious and her instinct when she felt this way was to leave.

As she rose from the table, he gently put his hand upon her arm. She felt a tingle.

"Will you be coming to mass next Sunday?"

"I don't know, maybe."

She looked down at him and found his brown eyes neither pleading nor demanding. He simply wanted to know if she'd return.

"OK, sure," she said.

"Outstanding," he replied with a hint of enthusiasm as he rose.

She remembered that never in her life had a man risen when she did. He was a respectful man, as she had expected any man of God to be. Maybe this wasn't out of the ordinary, and thinking this made her feel silly for taking note of a small gesture that caused such an instant liking to him.

The next Sunday she again arrived a few minutes after the service had started and while he didn't make much of her entrance, she felt that he had noticed her. Was she correct in thinking that was a smile?

She sat nervously at the coffee shop after service that day. She sipped her coffee, alone and watched as he took great interest in the lives of the other parishioners. He was a caring man, very earnest, very compassionate and what certainly didn't hurt, very handsome. She had finished her second cup of coffee and decided that maybe she should leave, maybe leave well enough alone. He was kind to her, she knew, because that's the type of person he was. He couldn't see her as she saw him, couldn't feel the same things, she thought, would never feel the same, so she decided against further action. She quickly consumed the rest of her coffee and got up to leave.

"You're not leaving, are you?"

He was standing close to her now. She could feel the nervousness come over her again. She wanted to leave, wanted to do anything but look into his eyes, but she found she could not resist his gaze.

"Well, I was, but I guess I could stay awhile."

"Splendid," he smiled as he sat down with her.

"Your coffee cup is empty. May I refill it?"

"No thank you," she said. "I've had two cups already."

"Good thing you got to it while it was hot," he smiled. "I've been walking around talking to the congregation with the same cold cup of coffee for thirty minutes!"

"Then let me get you a fresh cup."

She rose, stepped closer to him and reached for his cup. When she took possession of the cup, their fingers brushed together. She paused a moment and watched as his forefinger lingered on her hers. Was this really happening? He smiled as she nervously pulled the cup from his hands and for a second she was frozen. Those eyes! She stared breathlessly at him until she thought her heart might explode if she held that gaze much longer. As she snapped back to reality, she found that she had dropped the cup onto the floor, causing it to shatter into many pieces; tiny, white islands amidst a sea of black.

"Oh God, I'm so sorry," she cried.

"Nonsense."

"I just, I just…"

"Please," he said, taking her hand in his and motioning for her to sit down. "Perhaps it was a sign."

"A sign?"

"Yes, maybe God is telling me something."

"What?"

"That maybe perhaps I need to cut back on the caffeine!"

His laughter was soft, his smile broad. She found herself laughing too. His manner put her at ease and they talked like that for hours, long after the last parishioner had walked to their table and bid farewell and God bless.

She walked further on down the street as the low sodium street lamps struggled to turn on. There was no one out at this time, though it was not late. Weeknights in this part of town were always dead, with nowhere for people to go. There were no clubs, no bars, no restaurants; nothing around but the old coffee house and the decaying warehouses with their crumbling brick facades flanking both sides of the street.

It didn't occur to her that it might not be safe to walk this part of town alone. She felt a presence lately, something that moved her on, gave her strength each morning, though she had no idea what it was, nor did she even question this new strength.

She walked past an abandoned grocery store and was reminded of the Church's food drive she had once volunteered for. She had volunteered, mostly because he would be there and as long as she could be near him, she had bargained with herself, that it would be enough. She stayed late into many evenings counting the donations of food, canned and otherwise and divided them into piles for each package to be delivered the next day to needy families. She told herself she did this because she cared, which was true, but it was also because she would be able to at last steal long looks at him without incurring the suspicions of the other volunteers.

On the last evening of the food drive, he noticed that she was the last volunteer there. He had told her she should go on home many times, but she kept working. She wanted to complete every box so that every family was taken care of. And she wanted to impress him.

She had finished packing the last box, written the last address on it and taped it closed. She was almost sorry that the last box was finished, but she felt such a sense of satisfaction in completing the job long after everyone else had gone home.

She loaded the last box onto the pallet and looked around for the priest. He was busy mopping the floor around the production area. She was touched by this, by his willingness to do the little things. There was a janitor employed by the Church, but he'd said that the mess was his and his to clean up.

She busied herself tidying up where she could, delaying her departure as long as she dared. When she had done enough and didn't wish to trouble the priest any longer, she went over to bid him goodnight. She took two steps onto the wet floor, lost her balance, and the next thing she knew her head was being cradled in the priest's lap.

"Thank God you're alright. You are alright, aren't you?"

"I think so. What happened?"

"You slipped and hit your head on the floor."

"I am such a klutz."

"No, it was my fault. I was thinking that maybe I should put up one of those wet floor signs and the next thing I hear is this thud."

"I was just coming by to say good night."

"I'm so sorry."

"It's ok."

"I wish I had some ice, you've got quite a bump. I checked in the fridge, but every ice cube tray was empty."

"It's ok, really I'm fine," she said rubbing her head and trying to get up.

"Maybe you should lay still."

"No, I need to get up."

She sat up and turned to him. She felt around on her scalp and found she had a large bump at the back of her head. She shook her head and laughed.

"What's so funny?" he inquired.

"I'm so klutzy."

"No, not at all. Had you slipped on a dry floor, then yes, you'd definitely be klutzy."

She laughed at his remark and felt the throbbing of her head for the first time. He saw her wince and as she placed a hand over the bump, the priest gently placed his hand on her cheek. He smiled slightly less now, more out of concern than of mirth. He leaned in close to check her eyes, make sure her pupils weren't dilated. She saw the tenderness in his eyes, felt it in his touch. She couldn't help

172

herself now as she slightly closed her eyes and leaned into him with lips parted.

His eyes lost their focus now. She saw him look down at her lips, at her nose and her eyes again. His hands paused on her cheek. She could feel his breath caressing her lips, a prelude to such wonderment. She felt as if her heart might stop beating as she felt his lips brush so gently against hers.

Then he stopped. He pulled back with a look of confusion of his face.

"I'm sorry," he managed to say calmly, though he was obviously shaking.

He stood up and looked nervously around the room. Satisfied that no one was here at this hour, that no one had witnessed anything, he bent over, took her hand and lifted her up.

He walked her to the bus stop in time to catch the last bus. He had told her that he would take her to the hospital, but she refused. He bid her an awkward goodbye and stayed until she had found a seat. She saw through the window that he had stayed as the bus pulled away, his gaze fixated on her, watching her until the bus turned a corner and then he was gone.

She reached up now to feel the scar on her head that remained from that night. It gave her comfort sometimes, to feel that scar, to run her fingers over it and imagine that it were his fingers that she felt.

She smiled quietly to herself as she reached the street corner. She turned left and continued towards her destination, feeling every step upon the hard sidewalk.

She thought back again, these memories keeping her warm in her walk. She thought about her last confession, on a night just like this one, except it had been raining. She thought about how she had slipped into the confessional

173

booth quietly as the time allowed was ending, not knowing what she would say to him.

She listened to his greeting through the dark screen, and she suddenly found she couldn't concentrate on what she wanted to say, on what she had rehearsed; she was lost in the sounds of his voice.

"May the Lord be with you," he said.

"Hi," she said feebly.

"What are the sins you wish to confess?"

What was it she wanted to say? That she felt love for him, that she felt desire? That her sin was the dream of being with him, of holding him close to her, feeling his nakedness against hers?

She felt delirious, felt confused now as she tried to control the millions of thoughts that ran through her head. She was mad at herself for coming here, mad for feeling the way she did.

"Anger," she said at last.

"In what ways were you angry?"

"At myself."

"In what way?"

"At wanting something I cannot have."

"Is it covetous?"

She felt as though maybe he didn't recognize her voice. She thought maybe she should just finish up, make up something and get out of here. Her heart was pounding and her voice was wavering. She could hear now the slight quiver that disguised her voice when she spoke.

"I miss you," she finally blurted out.

"I'm sorry?"

"I miss you. You're all I think about."

Though she could no longer hear his voice, she could hear him moving about in the confessional. She had done it now, she thought, so why stop here.

"I love how you look at me," she said, waiting for a response and when none came, she cleared her throat and continued.

"I miss it, I really do. I even miss watching how kind you are to everyone, how even the littlest person matters greatly to you. You love people; you have so much capacity for love. I've never met a man like you. Most of them are callous and uncaring, but not you. I see great things in you and I feel like I matter when you look at me."

"Patricia," he began, "I cannot feel this for you."

"But you do, I know you do! I'm sorry, I know, I know this is wrong, how I feel, but I have to say this, I have to confess to this. If it is a sin to love a man of God, then I have sinned greatly. But I feel in my heart of hearts that this is not wrong, that this love I feel for you is true and just. I don't know what else to do and I couldn't tell you any other way. I'm sorry it had to be like this."

He didn't reply. It seemed like an eternity for her, sitting here in this wooden box lined in velvet, almost like a tomb. At last she heard his door open, listened to his few steps and felt the rush of cool air wash over her as he opened the door to her confessional.

He stood there for a moment, unsure of what to say. He seemed like he would fall over were it not for his white knuckled grip on the door.

"You are forgiven," he managed at last.

"That's it?"

"Yes."

"No 'Our Fathers' or 'Hail Mary's' to recite?"

"No."

"What then?"

"You must go."

He took her hand and helped her out of the booth, but he didn't follow her out, didn't stare after her. As she passed through the massive doors to the church, she looked back to see him still standing at the confessional, eyes fixed firmly on the floor.

She walked out into the rain, thankful for once for the downpour that masked her tears. She walked down the steps, cursing herself for being so stupid, for making such a fool of herself. So what if she loved him, so what if she felt this longing for him? Why couldn't she just keep this to herself? Did she really need to do this, to confess her feelings, to put it all out in the open to a man she could never have? Was she so selfish as to make her burden his burden?

She cursed out loud, cursed at herself as she descended the many steps to the street. She cursed herself as she walked to the bus shelter, believing that she'd made the greatest mistake of her life.

She stood there, replaying the moment while waiting for the bus. Why not just confess something else? Forgetting the Sabbath? Why even go? She tried to understand her motivation, but she felt drawn by something beyond her understanding. This felt right, was her answer, though she knew it to be wrong, this was the first time something ever felt this right.

At last the bus came and slowed to a stop as the doors swung open. She stared at her feet as she took the first step off the pavement and stepped onto the bus. Then she stopped. She looked up at the driver, as if looking for a sign. Make me get on this bus, she thought. Please make me.

"On or off, lady," was his reply.

She wasn't surprised when she found herself stepping off the bus.

"This is the last bus of the night, lady. Not the best neighborhood for a woman to be by herself."

She smiled at him and receded back into the shelter.

"Suit yourself," she heard him say as he swung the doors closed.

She watched as the bus disappeared down the street and then turned back toward the church.

She found the main door to the rectory unlocked. She passed unnoticed through the first floor, only the statuary were witness to her presence. She ascended the stairs to where she thought his room might be. She found the door easily; it was the only one with light slipping out from under the door. She gathered her nerve and approached the door. She lifted her fist to knock and froze.

She leaned close and listened. She heard nothing. She thought she might hear prayers, a murmured voice, pages of the good book turning, yet she heard nothing.

It was now or never, she thought, better get this done before the light goes out. She closed her eyes, took a deep breath and rapped gently on the door.

She braced herself for further admonition. She had been yelled at by men before, humiliated, beaten even. She heard the footsteps, heard the latch turning and in that moment, forgot what she was going to say.

The door opened slowly. For some reason she expected a calmly priest, relaxed and preparing for rest. She imagined a candle burning, a cup of tea cooling next to a bible, open to a favorite passage. She expected him to open the door with a kind look of concern, ready to assuage and forgive her childish delusions.

Instead she found him disheveled; his collar missing, his top two buttons not just undone, but torn away. His eyes were red and swollen. When she looked passed him to the table where she imagined such humble diversions, she saw a freshly opened fifth of bourbon.

She was about to apologize when he stepped forward and gently cupped her face in his hands. He then pulled her toward him, slowly and lightly pressed his forehead against hers. She closed her eyes, lost in the moment, her breath becoming shallow. She felt his face pull away from her and she opened her eyes.

She expected him to taste like liquor when he finally pulled her close and kissed her. Instead, she tasted something fragrant and beautiful and the room exploded into a menagerie of colors, so brilliant and blinding and full of ambrosia.

She walked almost waltz like in her steps, reliving the evening of her recent past. She thought she could still smell him on her fingertips, smell the gentle fragrance that emanated from his hair, from his breath; the sweetness of his presence.

She eventually reached her destination, and passing through the automatic sliding doors brought her memories to a close. She kept the warmth of his embrace fresh in her mind; she would need it now more than ever.

She got off the elevator at the third floor and signed in with the attending nurse. She gowned up and walked eagerly to basinet number four.

"Hi precious! How is my beautiful baby girl?"

Beneath the many wires that connected the various parts of the body and despite the many tethers that science had created to monitor and supply life, all Patricia saw in that basinet was a baby girl, her daughter; a child born of love into a world full of doubt.

She reached in close and cradled the child in her hands, felt her warmth, knew she recognized her.

She leaned in close and pressed her lips gently against the side of the baby's head and lingered there for a moment.

She then softly placed the baby down and smiled at her. She knelt by the resting baby and began to pray. Not of a cure, for her daughter was dying and there was nothing she or the doctors could do about it. She prayed for the baby's father, that he may be able to see her, to know of her before she is called back into the hands of God.

Chapter 26

Erikson's shoes echoed as he and Eisen strode quickly over the suspended floor tiles. They hurried towards a room at the far corner of the IT floor.

"You're late," a voice called from behind a bank of computer terminals as they entered.

"It couldn't be helped," Erikson answered.

"Too bad, I'm outta here. I told you to be here an hour ago, but for some reason that was too difficult for you."

"Cut us a break, we had to interview a witness," Eisen said.

"Not interested," was the reply.

"Well," Erikson began, "we understand. This probably isn't for you. It might be too high tech; maybe it's

more up Ferguson's ally. He's on tomorrow morning, right?
I think he's better qualified for this sort of thing, anyway."

The man stopped packing his messenger bag and
stared coldly at Erikson.

"Nobody rocks it like Francis Toombs."

"Then you'll help us," asked Erikson.

"Say it," Toombs demanded.

"Please?"

"'Nobody rocks it like Francis Toombs.'"

Erikson looked at Eisen, who was desperately trying
to stifle a smile.

"Nobody rocks it like Francois Toombs."

"Damn straight," Toombs said. "Now, let's begin."

Toombs dropped his bag onto the floor for effect,
then sat in his chair and began typing furiously. After
spending most of his efforts on streamlining software search
engines, mostly for DMV searches and fingerprints, and
trying to be nice while spending valuable time fixing user
errors so boneheaded it made him wince, he finally got
something worth his efforts. Still, he reasoned, these folks
needed to know who they were dealing with and where their
place was when they walked into his domain.

"This is what's so cool about it," Francis cooed as he
stopped typing, "take a look."

The two detectives crowded behind Toombs, staring
over his shoulder at the screen.

"What are we looking at?" asked Eisen.

"A thing of beauty. Check this out. This is the
tracking device that Erikson wanted me to find. This is one
really nice piece of surveillance equipment."

"You found it already?" Erikson asked.

"Who rocks it?" Toombs asked rhetorically, but
waited for an answer before proceeding.

"You rock it," Eisen jumped in, happy for any sign of good news.

"How?" Erikson asked.

"This thing's got a GPS. Sure, we can triangulate the position like a cell phone, but check this out; we can get a history on it. It records shit."

"I just want to know where it is," Eisen intoned.

"Oh, it'll tell you that," he said nodding his head, "it'll tell you the person's pulse, blood sugar, blood alcohol, all that shit."

"Where is it?"

"Patience, please! May I enjoy finally getting to do something worthy of my talents?"

"People's lives are at stake," Eisen said.

"Detective, what your partner has asked me to do isn't exactly legal. There's no warrant you can get for the shit I'm hacking into. I'm talking telecom satellites, real, real heavy shit here. Please show some reverence for the technology and respect for my abilities."

"What Detective Eisen meant," Erikson interrupted, "is that while we're awed by what you've done for us, and it is amazing, we need to get the answers in a more timely fashion."

"Fine," Francis said, turning away and frantically typing at his keyboard.

"First, it was damaged," he continued. "I don't know how, because I don't know the hardware of this device. It's custom, no doubt. I have the initial location, at the hospital, and then it goes dead."

"Dead?" Eisen asked. "So that's it?"

"Hold on," Francis said as he slid his chair over to an adjacent terminal and began furiously punching in code.

182

"And here, it reappears. It sends a distress signal, a ping. This must be where it was removed, but the time signature is off."

"What are you talking about, time signature? What does that mean?" Erikson asked, leaning in close over his shoulder to try and discern the mysterious code that Francis was translating.

"Well, it has two signatures for the distress ping signal. This means that someone was trying to mask it. Then it goes dead, then reboots several hours later. Don't ask me how, but somebody knew how to blanket the device. Not an easy thing to do let me tell you."

He wheeled his chair back to his main computer and punched at the keyboard for a few seconds.

"Here I found it. Funny location. Do you know where it is?"

Erikson looked onto the map on the screen and shook his head.

"That's a landfill."

"Great," Eisen said loudly.

"Now hold on," Francis demanded. "This is where it is at this moment. When I traced its history back using the GPS signal and triangulation, I found that at one point it was synonymous with the global position of one of the trash trucks. I snuck a look at their servers. Man, what a fucking joke. That security needs a serious upgrade! Just like hotwiring a GM in high school!"

He laughed out loud until he caught Eisen glaring at him. He shifted in his chair and pointed a long, thin finger at the screen.

"Ok, the earliest that these two signals coincided was here."

"That's a mighty broad area," Erikson added.

"Yeah, no joke. But check this out. Since this is an old industrial area with many abandoned buildings, I ran a search with the utility company to see which buildings were still drawing power. I got this one. Might be nothing, but then again, it's the closest time signature that could match one of the signals."

"Beautiful," Erikson cheered as Francis handed him the address.

Francis smiled broadly and waited for Eisen to acknowledge his genius. She feigned a miserable smile and walked away. Erikson pocketed the slip of paper that bore the address and followed his partner. When he neared the door, he heard Francis clear his throat loudly.

"Detective Erikson?"

Erikson turned around and raised his eyebrows, trying to pretend he didn't know what was wanted of him, but knowing full well his ruse wasn't working.

"Our agreement?"

"Yes."

"Saturday?"

"I'll be there."

"Excellent."

Chapter 27

Eisen parked the car down the block from the address that Toombs had derived. The street was broad, with broken cobble stones left unmaintained long enough that weeds were growing through.

"Got a cigarette?" Eisen asked. "And please, no sermon."

"You know what," Erikson answered as he pulled the pack of smokes and his lighter out and handed them to Eisen, "keep 'em."

"I just want one."

"No keep 'em. Fuck it, I'm quitting. This way, you won't smoke because you won't be able to bum them off me."

"I only want one."

"Nope. All or nothing. And keep the lighter."

"Thanks. It's the red brick one up ahead on the right," Eisen said as she lit up a cigarette and proceeded to get out of the car.

"Wow, very nice. With a lot of work, this could qualify as one of those new urbanism areas. These are beautifully designed brick buildings."

"Yeah, yeah, yeah, less talk, more walk," Eisen said.

"You know how much a loft in a neighborhood like this would fetch in a city like New York or 'Frisco?"

"A lot?"

"Yeah," he replied, matching her sarcasm, "a lot!"

"So this is the result of the 'supposedly illegal activity' you thought was more important than our lead at the coffee shop? Maybe whoever got this device off the priest simply dumped it here."

"No, this is the result of a definitely illegal activity. Or, you could call it some damn fine police work. Either way, at least it got us something to go on."

"That woman at the coffee shop was something to go on."

"She has no clue where he is and he hasn't tried to contact her. I think this is a much better bet."

"And I'll bet that someone dumped the device here to throw us off."

"Look, I've invested quite a bit to get this information."

"What did it cost you?"

"I have to help him move."

"Wow. That's huge. I mean, even moving a friend is a big deal, right?"

"Unless they have beer."

"He's got beer?"

"He doesn't drink."

"Ouch," Eisen said, clearly empathizing with her partner.

"So, please, at least humor me. Let's check this out."

"Given what you have to do, for your sake, let's hope this lead turns up something."

They carefully made their way among the broken cobble stones and wayward vegetation. They took note of all the places that they could be spied upon through the fractured windows and found themselves very much in the open. They took note of every closed door, many of them padlocked from the outside. They nodded to each other when they felt they had noticed a dangerous spot that could conceal a shooter. If someone didn't want them to be here, Erikson knew, there wasn't much they could do about it now.

Unbeknownst to each other, they each breathed a sigh of relief when they arrived at the address. Despite the neighborhood being in various states of decay, the building at this address appeared in better shape than its neighbors. The building was dirty, but they found as they climbed the steps to the main entrance, that it was free of debris; no broken bottles or trash blocking their path.

Erikson took note that the door was not padlocked like the others. Upon closer inspection, he found that the door had no lock at all. He looked back at Eisen, shrugged and pushed slowly. The door eased open a few inches.

"After you," Eisen whispered.

"Gee, Thanks."

Erikson stepped forward and pressed his shoulder against the door. He pushed further, opening the door enough to see there was a dimly lit corridor that terminated about twenty feet ahead. They both slipped inside and closed the door so that it made no sound.

They could see fairly well and made their way down the short corridor. As they reached the end, they found themselves before a magnificently decorated door. It appeared odd that a door of such decoration would be in a place like this, standing guard at the end of a non-descript hallway highlighted with studs that shown through the damaged lathe and plaster walls.

Eisen ran her hands along the door's surface and found it very uneven. She drew her handgun and operated the light on the underside. She was surprised by the intricate artwork etched into its surface. With her free hand, she continued searching for a handle or other means by which to open the door, but found none. While it did not appear to have any locking mechanism, she couldn't figure out how to open it.

"Can't get it opened?" Erikson chided.

"Are you sure this is a door?" Eisen asked, sounding frustrated.

"Let's see," Erikson said, easing Eisen aside.

He pulled out a flashlight and illuminated where he ran his hand around the perimeter of the door and was surprised to find that the bottom of the door was flush against the floor. No light or air could be perceived form the other side.

"Hmm, that's odd," Erikson said.

"What?" asked Eisen.

"The door is resting on the floor."

"Is it broken? Off the hinges?"

"No, no hinges, not that I can find on this side. A door this large would create a great deal of friction on the floor if it were expected to swing, but there are no swing marks, so that's out."

"It swings in?"

"Can't. The door protrudes six inches out on either side."

"So how does it open, then?" Eisen wondered. "Does it slide, raise, what?"

"I don't know. I've never seen anything like it. It's got to be, what, eight feet high and as wide across. And as it's made of heavy timber, I doubt, wait…"

"What?"

"Look, at the center, there's some kind of inscription. Can you see it?"

"Vaguely. What does it say?"

"I don't know. It's not in English."

"Latin, maybe?"

"Could be. Can you read Latin?"

"Not a bit," Eisen said. "You?"

"I took it in high school, so I should know a few words. Mind you, I got a C-," he joked as he blew the dust from the inscription. "OK, here goes; Fourth word is 'Porta,' which is door, so I'm guessing maybe it explains how to open it, but the rest, let's see, there's," he paused for a minute before continuing, "Nope, that's it. I got 'door'."

"You think you can figure out how to open it somehow?"

"Yeah, as soon as these other words come back to me," Erikson answered.

"Well, you work on that and I'm going to see if there's some other way in," Eisen said as she switched off her light and holstered her weapon. "There has to be. A building this size can't just have a street entrance that leads to a short corridor that terminates at this thing. I'm going to go around the alley to the rear, maybe find a way in there. I'll radio you if I get in and you do the same if you can figure out how to get this open."

"I don't think we should split up."

189

"I'll be fine. You just get this door open in case I find nothing out back."

"I'll do my best."

Chapter 28

Eisen paused as she stepped out of the building. The street was vacant; no cars, no people. This is how she expected to find it, but she was still mindful of the many dangers that such an environment can conceal.

She began counting her steps and walked towards the end of the block, which was one more large brick warehouse away. When she was a good twenty feet past their building, she looked up towards the windows on the second and third floors. From this angle, the windows reflected the sky perfectly, allowing her no vision to the inside. She knew she would have to cross the street for a good view, but she would also be opening herself up as well.

She continued to the corner, turned and walked to the alley that ran along the rear of the buildings. She paused to take in the sight lines, possible blind spots that could mask a threat. So as not draw attention, she discretely slid her weapon from its holster, held it pressed against her hip and began walking down the center of the alley.

She counted down her steps now, wanting to make sure that she could find the right building. She knew that the rear of these buildings blended together, that it was often difficult to tell where one building ended and another began. The last thing she needed to be doing was wasting precious time rummaging through the wrong building.

When she had counted off her steps, she felt justified in her efforts, since she was now looking at a straight, unbroken brick façade that extended thirty feet past where she had stopped and all the way back to the mouth of the alley.

She looked up, taking in the approximate height of the building. This appeared the same at the front. However, she found the windows in the rear were boarded up. She saw that every window, on both sides of the alley, was closed off in this fashion.

Eisen did find an overhead door and a side door aligned with her building. She walked to the steps along the concrete loading dock; she found them cracked and broken with rusted strands of rebar exposed to the elements. She climbed carefully, as there were no handrails and she didn't trust that the steps would hold, but they did and she found herself in front of the overhead door. She saw now that the door was padlocked on each side, with the locks showing the same rust as the rebar in the concrete. She reasoned that this door hasn't been opened in a great many years.

She had no better luck with the side door. Although it appeared to be unlocked, it had a padlock as well which would only allow the door to open an inch when she pushed on it. She lifted the padlock, feeling the gritty surface rust that the years had wrought. For kicks, she pulled heavily on the padlock and was surprised when it opened.

She removed the lock and carefully pushed the door open, using the heavy steel door as a shield. She raised her weapon and turned on its light and peered into the room. She saw it was completely devoid of furniture but littered with debris. When she was certain it was safe to enter, she slipped inside and eased the door closed behind her.

As her eyes adjusted, she found a solitary door at the back of the room. As she stepped towards it, she heard Erikson on her radio. Though she had the volume on its lowest setting, the sound of his voice echoed loudly in the empty room.

"Eisen," she heard him call.

"I'm here," she whispered.

"I think I got it figured out."

"Great. I'm inside too, in what seems to be a small office just off the shipping dock out back."

"You need to come and see this. This is amazing. All I have to do is…"

Erikson's voice cut out as the building was rocked by an explosion, sending Eisen crashing to the floor. She struggled to get up, feeling the aftershock resonate through the heavy timber floor. Finally, after great effort, she found herself on her feet.

She had kept possession of her weapon, managed to keep it firmly in her hand without discharging a shot as she fell. The same could not be said for her radio, which had flown from her grasp and was now lost among the debris.

She ran to the door at the rear of the room, but found this locked. She threw herself against it, but it would not move. She turned and ran out the door from which she entered, ran along the length of the dock and jumped into the alley, hitting the ground at full stride.

As she turned the corner to the street, she saw smoke escaping from the main door of the building. She ran to it and flung it open and was met by a wall of smoke, thick and black. She crouched as she stepped inside and crawled along the floor, trying to keep from choking as she hurried towards her partner.

She moved quickly, against the wall, feeling the floor begin to tilt. Because she couldn't see, she couldn't keep herself from sliding towards the hole in the floor, couldn't manage to grab onto anything, to keep her from falling into the darkness below.

When she came to, she found herself laying on a soft, dirt floor. She looked up to see the hole from which she had fallen. The light coming from above, though meager, allowed her to locate her weapon, which had landed a few feet away from her.

Eisen got up, dusted herself off and picked up her weapon. She pulled the clip, checked it, replaced it and pulled the slide to free anything that might impede the action. She knocked on the light, hoping it would come back on.

She was relieved that it still worked. She readied herself and set off to find a way out. There was only one, she found, a door; and it was locked from the outside. She moved around quickly now to find anything she could use. She hoped to find some rope, but there was none. She figured that it was maybe at least ten feet from floor to floor. She knew she couldn't jump high enough to grasp one of the joists that the explosion had exposed. She had to find something to stand on.

She shone the light around the room and found a few crates, made from slats of wood. Eisen holstered her weapon and dragged the two crates under the opening above. She stacked the crates on top of each other and climbed very carefully until she was balancing on the top crate. She reached up and could almost get her fingers around the joist. She pressed down with her legs and sprang upwards, just managing to get a decent hold on the joist as the crates cracked and gave way.

She held on, knowing that if this failed, there was no other way out of this room. And without her radio, she might be down here a very long time. She hoped that someone might have noticed the explosion, but now that the smoke had cleared and no one was here, she felt very much alone. She began to shake as she clung to the joist, feeling fear for the first time as her adrenaline wore off.

But she had no choice. She could climb out, or most likely stay here to die.

She pulled herself up, steadied herself enough so that she could reach one arm out flat on the edge of the floor and managed to get herself up and onto the joist. She crawled along the joist towards the edge of the floor and threw herself against the wall when she was clear. She noticed how she gasped for breath as she sat against the far wall.

When she was calm, she took a moment to assess the surroundings and she found them odd; the corridor was clean. There were no signs that an explosion had taken place; the massive wooden door was gone, giving way to a jagged opening in the wall, but there was no debris. There were neither shards nor pieces of the door. The walls appeared wiped down, as there was little soot or signs of smoke damage. And Eisen noticed, sitting here on the floor, that it had been mopped. What more, there were no signs of her partner. No body, no blood: nothing.

She got up and slid herself against the wall, not trusting the floor whose width exposed more of the pit as she walked on.

When she came to where the massive door had been, she knew that it had been used to keep trespassers from entering, but from what? The room looked beyond clean. If they had time to clean the mess from the blast, she thought, they certainly could have cleared this room. Such a deadly door must be used to keep something secret. She drew her weapon, pressed herself against the broken wall and turned quickly into the room.

She held her weapon ready, not quite sure that she wouldn't have to use it. She scanned the room several times, back and forth, up and down, before entering. She pressed on, farther into the room, looking over the sight of her gun as she moved forward.

The room was massive; at least as wide as the structure and maybe thirty feet to the back wall, which didn't go all the way up to the exposed structure above. There was one door and as she approached it, she found it to be ajar.

Inside this room, she found a sofa, velvet and thread bare, with wood trim, positioned on a very large Oriental rug, keeping company with two large wingback chairs.

Though she had been trained to be cautious, Eisen moved hurriedly through the space. She knew she had to find her partner, but even more important, had to salvage something, save something from the abyss she felt forming from the fear that he was dead.

She made it through this room in a few seconds. She arrived at a large sliding medal dock door at the rear. While this one was similar in size to the rigged ornamental door, this one did not have any ornamentation but it did have a latch. Though it was unlocked, the latch made a very loud and distinct sound as she released it and Eisen grimaced, expecting the worst.

With the door open, she found herself in a loading bay, with the large exterior overhead door to the outside loading dock directly ahead of her. To her right, she identified the door to the shipping office she couldn't previously open and on her left of this empty space she saw a corridor that led to a staircase. She crossed quickly to the corridor and paused at the stairs. One flight led straight up to a well lit landing. The other led straight down into the darkness from which she had earlier escaped. This flight offered no end in sight, just dozens of steps that were devoured by the darkness; a place she did not wish to revisit.

Floors at ground level and above are somewhat predictable, she'd been taught at the academy. Cellars and levels deep under the ground have little rhyme or reason, especially in older structures. Think of tunnels, she'd learned; know your way or wait for backup.

She readied herself and began to ascend the staircase. She hoped that she had chosen the right path, as the other one terrified her. She hoped with each step that she would find Erikson somewhere upstairs, quite possibly injured, but hopefully alive. She tried to push from her mind the worst case, the thought that kept screaming in her mind to be heard; that he was dead and his remains were hidden, locked in some dark, forsaken part of the cellar.

"Please be alive, be ok," she whispered to herself as she reached the end of the long flight of steps.

At the top of the stairs, she was able to see directly down a narrow corridor. Two doors on each side, both of them shut, nothing but darkness within. Directly ahead, at the end of the hall, she saw a third door, slightly open, light coming forth. She pressed herself against the wall to her right as she walked slowly now, toward the first door to the right.

She knew not to enter this room. Entering a dark room with light at your back was suicide, as was standing so the silhouette of your legs showed underneath, so she leapt as best she could and cleared the threshold.

She picked up her pace now, gaining speed to clear the next threshold more easily, landing a good two feet beyond the door.

She was now a few feet away from the room at the end of the hall. She crept forward; stopping every few feet to listen for any voices, any sign of conversation, but all was quiet save for the pounding of her heart.

When she reached the open door, she peered cautiously through the opening into the room. She was surprised by the grandeur of the décor. She had expected debris, maybe, or a disheveled office, even, but interiors such as this were found in mansions. Somebody lived here, and lived well. She quietly checked the action of her gun, making sure she had previously chambered a round.

She swung her gun in quickly, pushing the door open. She searched over the sights for any movement, and then entered into the room, keeping tight against the wall to her left.

As her breathing calmed, she realized she was standing in a large bedroom. There were exquisite tapestries of ancient events on the walls, covering the exposed brick. The largest was a portrait of a crusader on horseback, with the sun at his back and angels circling him as he rode forth. The others were likely more detailed, but she couldn't risk the distraction of each one's splendor as she moved further into the room.

She passed by a desk with nothing on it; no pens, no paper, no sign of use. She reached down to the top drawer and quietly slid it open. Inside were several papers in a language she didn't understand. She could pick out French, Italian, German and Spanish in written form, but this one was wholly foreign.

After leafing through the papers, she carefully slid the drawer closed and moved on towards a series of bookcases nearby, arranged as if in a library, but angled just enough to conceal a threat. She managed to get alongside the first stack without noise, but as she swept out at the corner to gain visual advantage of the second stack, she unwittingly clipped a large tome and sent it to the floor.

The large book landed with its full weight flat on its cover. The concussion it made upon impact reverberated like a gunshot, causing Eisen to spin back and take cover behind the stacks. She held her breath and closed her eyes, swearing repeatedly at herself.

For a full minute, all she could hear was the sound of the book, but when her breathing returned to normal, she could make out what she thought was a voice. She quietly moved to the edge of the stack in the direction of the sound.

As she neared the end of the bookcase, she could make out the sound.

"Eisen?"

It was calling her name, but the voice sounded strange and distant. She got to her knees and leaned against the edge of the stack of books. From this vantage point, she would be able to see anyone coming before they could discern her location. She could also see the headboard of a large and magnificent bed, bigger than any she had ever seen. It was much larger than a king size bed, and the wood work was vast; there didn't seem to be an inch of it that wasn't intricately carved.

"Eisen?"

The voice sounded calm, as if simply asking for her attention.

She thought it could be a trap, someone calling her name and when she came into view, she'd be shot dead. Instinct told her not to risk it, but no, she thought, why would they first give themselves away? From the sound of the voice she figured that whoever was calling her was on the other side of the headboard. They had to know that she had the advantage of position, as long as she stayed put.

"Eisen?"

This time, the voice was louder, but no more urgent. She leaned forward and decided this is it. She stood up and followed the direction of her firearm which she pointed toward the massive bed. She paused as she reached the headboard which was a full foot taller than she. She braced for whatever would happen next and swung her weapon around the corner, prepared to fire if necessary.

She looked down and found a figure wrapped in cloth, resting on the center of the bed. The figure was covered from head to toe, in beautiful strips of ivory cloth. The cloth was bright enough in the sunlight to create a stark contrast against the white linen sheets.

She released her left hand from the gun and pulled at the strips of cloth around the figure's head. As they slid effortlessly off the skull, she could almost make out the profile. She put her gun on the bed next to the head and, unencumbered now, quickly began to pull the bandages free. As she pulled more swaths from the mouth, the breathing became louder, but not labored.

"Eisen?"

"Erikson," she exclaimed, excited and relieved to finally find her partner. "Don't worry, I'll get you free. They've got you wrapped up somehow. "

"Eisen, I can't move," he said.

She was surprised that he didn't sound frightened. If anything, he sounded calm.

"Shhh, quiet."

"No, its ok," he assured her.

As she pulled another swath of bandages from his head, she heard the floorboards behind her creak. In one smooth, fluid motion, she grabbed her gun and wheeled around and leveled it at the head of a man standing behind her.

"Don't move," Eisen ordered.

"It's he who shouldn't move," the man offered calmly as he resumed his steps and walked around Eisen towards the foot of the bed.

"Freeze, goddamit," Eisen ordered.

"You won't shoot me."

"Want to bet?"

"Would you be willing to bet your friend's life? If so, feel free to shoot. However, I am the only one who can finish healing him."

"Who are you?"

"My name is Mac."

"What did you do to him?" Eisen asked over the gun still trained at the man's head.

"If you please, Detective Eisen, lower your weapon. It's of no use here."

Eisen lowered her weapon slightly and relaxed her stance, but still held the gun on the man.

"Very well then," Mac shrugged and went about soaking more strips in a bowl of clear liquid, then applying those strips of the elegant cloth to Erikson.

"We need to get him to a hospital," Eisen demanded.

"We are saving his life."

"Hey," Eisen said loudly, trying to get Mac's attention, shaking the gun at him for added effect. "You tried to kill him!"

"The door was booby-trapped. It was essentially meant to be able to kill up to five men with the blast. However, the explosive material is quite old so he's very lucky that little of it detonated. We never thought anyone would be clever enough to figure out how to open it."

"So I should thank you after all this?"

"Not me. I desire no thanks. Your partner is alive because of my Master."

"You have a master?"

"Yes."

"Where is he?"

"It is quite impossible to disturb him right now."

"I say otherwise," she said, shaking the gun.

"I must apologize, but that is strictly forbidden."

Eisen cocked the gun and tried to call his bluff but he stood up straight, raised his head and offered her a smile.

"If you are going to kill me, please, do not hesitate further. Otherwise, allow me to lend assistance to your friend."

"Alright then," she said, finally lowering the weapon to her side, "is he going to live?"

"Of course. Master can heal all wounds."

"What 'Master?' What are you talking about?"

"Eisen," she heard Erikson interrupt in a small voice, "it was beautiful. He took me into his arms and I felt such lightness and warmth, as if I entered a place in which fear never existed. I felt this all over my body."

"Who did this?" She asked him as she leaned close.

"I don't know, I didn't see his face, but I felt him, felt him as if I was him, as if he and I were one and the same, as if we shared the same body."

"He's delirious," she said to Mac as he finished attending to Erikson.

"Eisen," Erikson said now, in a hushed tone, "he's here."

Eisen's look begged the question.

"The priest," Erikson said.

202

Eisen had forgotten about finding this priest. He was, after all, the entire reason they were here, but now her partner's life was at stake, and that took priority.

"I'm gonna get you out of here."

"No, he must rest," Mac interrupted.

"If you've healed him, why are you wrapping him up like some mummy?"

"Master healed him, but he was very badly hurt. I'm merely speeding the recovery process. His body was torn apart. These strips of cloth are soaked with an ancient essence that will return his strength, but it takes time."

"And if you remove them?"

"He may die."

"I can't believe I'm hearing this bullshit."

"You should go," Mac said.

"I'm not leaving."

"You should not be here."

"You've got my partner wrapped up like fucking King Tut and you think I'm going to just walk away?"

"It would be best, for everyone."

Eisen raised her weapon again so she could see the man through its sights.

"Stop what you're doing. Unwrap him, now! Last chance," she commanded.

"Please," a voice from far off said, "don't."

Eisen spun around and trained the gun on a figure emerging from a darkened alcove across the room. At first she couldn't believe she had missed this location, but shook it off and focused on this new threat.

"Get your hands up on top of your head and come out slowly now."

The figure that emerged from the shadows was Father Donovan.

"Well, well, well, the good Father," Eisen chimed sarcastically, "we've been looking for you."

"I know."

"In fact, you're the reason my partner is in this condition."

"On the contrary," Mac interrupted, "he's the reason your partner is still alive."

"You," she said turning her head slightly to Mac, "shut the fuck up. And you," she said, gun still on the priest, "you're coming with me. And you're going to carry Detective Erikson."

"I will go with you, but…"

"Father Donovan, that is forbidden," Mac said firmly.

"I will go with you," Donovan reiterated, "but your partner must stay. I know you do not believe, I did not at first, many months ago, but believe me, please believe me, there are great things at work here."

"Yeah, right, miracles? Let's go!"

"I'm sorry," Donovan said, "but he must stay."

"You're sorry? Fuck you, you're sorry! Maybe you're sorry that you got caught, maybe you're sorry for what you did to that poor woman, but no, I don't believe for a second you're sorry about my partner."

"What was that?"

"You heard me, now move!"

"No please, that part about the woman. What woman?" Donovan asked.

"Let's move, your holiness!"

Just as Eisen motioned with her gun for him to move, she felt pressure at the back of her head. Instantly she recognized that someone had snuck up behind her and was now pressing a gun against her skull.

"Drop gun, please," she heard a man with a thick accent say.

"I'm a police officer," she replied, "drop your weapon."

"I said, 'drop gun.' Please."

"I'd drop your weapon, Miss" Mac said. "He never says please."

"Slava, wait," Donovan interrupted, "please, she needs to tell me something."

"Three times, last time," Slava said, pushing the barrel even harder against her skull, "now please, drop gun or I kill you. Please."

"Ok," Eisen said, her grip loosening on her weapon so that the barrel rotated upward in her hand.

"Now drop," Slava said.

As Eisen bent over slightly to drop her weapon, she felt the pressure ease off the back of her skull. She knew the gun would be higher now, maybe above her head, so she took a chance. She dropped the weapon and as it made contact with the floor, she twisted sideways and threw an elbow to where she judged his solar plexus would be.

The blow was just enough to throw Slava off balance. He pulled the trigger, but he missed his intended target. As he staggered to right himself, he saw Mac staring at him, a dark spot beginning to blossom on his shirt. This distracted Slava enough to give Eisen time to take cover. She slid along the floor and propped herself up behind a massive timber column.

"Mac," Slava muttered as he stepped forward.

"No, it's ok," Mac stammered.

"Quick, we must get him to Judas," Donovan said, panic rising in his voice as he rushed over to Mac.

"No," Mac strained, "Master isn't ready. He's too weak. He hasn't rested enough."

205

"Slava, we've got to help him," Donovan pleaded.

"Mac, I carry you, give me hand," Slava said.

"No, there's nothing you can do. Nothing can be done. I've had enough, Slava. I'm tired. I can feel this, you know. I forgot what pain felt like. I'm so tired. Slava," Mac said, barely able to get the words out now. "Get Donovan out of here."

Slava bent down and retrieved Eisen's gun.

"Come," Slava said curtly, grabbing Donovan by the shoulder and dragging him along, "we must get you out of here."

"Slava wait," Donovan cried as he was yanked forward, "I have to know about the woman she spoke of. I have to hear her story."

"You want story? I tell you story," Slava yelled as he pulled the young priest from the room.

Chapter 29

Eisen swung around the column, her back up revolver in hand, leading the way. She watched the larger man drag Donovan back towards the dark alcove from which they came.

"Freeze," she screamed.

The larger man indeed froze, then much quicker than Eisen had anticipated, spun and fired at her. The bullet tore into the column inches above her head, splintered fragments exploding around her.

When she looked out again, the men were gone. She quickly made it over to her partner to check on him, but he was unconscious now. She tried removing the bandages around his neck to check his pulse when she felt a warm hand gently stop her efforts. Mac sat leaning against the bed, blood pooling about him.

"It is to be expected. You needn't worry, he will be fine."

"I'll get you an ambulance," she said to Mac. "Can you hold on?"

"Death isn't the worst thing that can happen to you, Detective Eisen. What happens to me right now is inconsequential. I have fulfilled my role, made my contributions. I feel as though I have done so much good, despite the bad. I do not fear death."

She stared at Mac, unable to find anything to say in response to this.

"I'll be back," she said as she squeezed her partners shoulder. Still starring at Mac, she hurried off into the darkened alcove.

"Please," Mac called after her, straining to get the words out, "watch out for Slava. Be very careful. Killing is all he knows."

In the alcove, she found a narrow staircase and followed the steps down. From her estimation, the steps didn't stop at the first floor, nor was there any landing; the steps just kept going. The light sconces ahead were out, or recently broken and the steps, just like the ones inside the loading dock, descended straight into darkness.

She was descending quickly into the bowels of the building. She had no light now, as the only one she carried was attached to her main gun and she had surrendered that one. She slowed her decent so her eyes could adjust to the darkness.

She could tell she was in the subterranean part of the building now by the dank smell of rot and decay. When she finally reached the bottom, she wasn't at all surprised to find the floor was dirt.

She felt around on the adjacent wall for a light switch, but couldn't find one.

She closed her eyes, hoping they would finally adjust to the darkness quicker. Then a thought occurred to her; she had Erikson's cigarettes and his lighter. She fumbled inside her jacket pocket for the lighter, pulled it out but dropped it into the dirt floor. She dropped down on all fours and swept her hands through the cold dirt until she found it. She then knocked it against her thigh to dislodge any debris, flipped it open and lit it.

She found that she was standing in a large, round vestibule, maybe twenty feet across. As she moved the lighter around, she saw fragments on the ground ahead of her reflecting the light. She bent down and picked up one of the larger, very thin pieces. It was the glass of an incandescent light bulb and she guessed that by how the shards lay on top of the dirt that they must have recently been broken. She stood up and raised the lighter and saw what was left of the stumble light; protective metal cover bent, the bulb destroyed.

She looked down again and could just make out two sets of foot prints going towards a door to her right. She walked outside the prints and pressed the back of her hand against the door. It felt cool to the touch. She slid her hand around on the steel surface and felt it move, but found no handle, latch or locking mechanism.

She inhaled and held her breathe for a few seconds, closed the lighter, then slowly pushed the door open a few inches. She saw light and felt a cool breeze, carrying with it that dank smell of earth. She then pulled her hand away and stepped back as the door came slowly and quietly to a close.

She readied her revolver and stood at the hinged side and pushed the door open with more force. This time, the door opened a few feet, more light piercing into the vestibule. She could see in the room maybe ten feet. She saw many large objects, all covered with canvas or similar type cloths and tied at the base with rope. She craned her head to see further, but the door was closing again. She put her hand out and stopped it. She pushed it open a little more and quickly entered the room, coming to a halt behind a large covered object.

This room was quite large, much larger than she would have thought in a cellar. From what she could tell, it was one hundred feet to the opposite wall, which housed the only source of illumination; one dirty, wire-reinforced clerestory window running the width of the room, about twelve feet from the floor. Unless this guy can get some air, there's no way out for him, she thought. If he's in here, he must be hiding somewhere amongst the mysterious covered objects.

Eisen realized that she had the advantage of the light from the windows being before her. This way, she would cast no shadow as she went forward. She crouched low at the base of one object, looking for her advantage in the guise of the shadow of a pair of legs. What she saw puzzled her. She saw before her dozens of pairs of legs. She moved quietly from her spot to the next object five feet ahead of her.

This object was not secured at the bottom. She lifted the canvas slightly and peered underneath. In the dim light she realized that she was looking at a statue of a man.

Some were on bases, some directly on palettes, some supported by vertical columns coming from the palettes, but all of them identically bound. She knew it would be impossible to get a shortcut; she'd have to go row by row and hopefully not become a target.

She thought about her partner and how she felt responsible for his predicament. However, even through the guilt that she felt, she couldn't help but feel somewhat abandoned here. Sure, it wasn't his fault he was clinging to life up there, victimized further by being forcibly bound. She recognized that she was his only hope of getting out of here to a hospital, getting the help he needed and now there was a feeling creeping up her spine, causing the hairs of the back of her neck to stand, that she might be of no aid at all to her partner if she were to die down here.

She took a deep breath and forced the thought from her mind. She'd be of no use to anyone focusing on past mistakes and winding up dead. She forced herself into action, pure physicality and she moved quickly toward the statue in the next row. She paused and strained to listen, but heard nothing. She stepped forward just as the statue she was behind exploded, shards and chunks of marble raining down under the canvas that had ballooned open from the force of the shot.

"To the right, to the right, go, go," she thought as she ran forward now, skipping the next row. She looked to the right and thought she had a bead on one of the men, but he was obscured by the unsecured drape of the canvas.

She knew better than to shoot at a target she couldn't fully identify. Yes, she knew it was one of the men, but was it the dangerous one with the gun, or the priest that they were looking for? She knew to count both as threats, but one was greater, and that was the target she knew she had to locate. She could make out the legs from mid calf down, but the shoes were obscured in the dirt floor. The larger man's feet must be larger, but now there was no way to tell.

She cocked the hammer and as she pulled the trigger, she remembered something she heard from her father when she was a child.

"A hunter was in the woods tracking deer through a dense thicket. This was back when red was the safety

211

color," she heard his voice clearly. "It was a hot day in late fall and this hunter decided to take off his coat. Underneath, he had on a white tee shirt and no sooner had he shed his outer layer when another hunter, seeing only the white of the tee shirt through the thicket, mistaking it for the tail of a deer, placed a round right into the man's chest. A perfect shot, right through the heart. Always identify your target, and take your time."

But time she didn't have. She had a target and knew it might be her only chance. As she aimed her gun, statues began exploding around her in a circular pattern attempting to pen her in. She squeezed off a round and suddenly the firing stopped.

The man behind the statue lurched forward, grabbing at the canvas cloth for support as he lost his balance. The heavy cloth, unrestrained by any rope, slid freely about the statue and finally came off as the man fell to his knees.

The man struggled to stay on his knees as he fought the heavy cloth that enveloped him. Eisen cautiously moved forward, gun still at the ready. When she got within twenty feet, she ordered the man to drop his weapon. The man still struggled with the cloth. She aimed her weapon; arms outstretched and hammer cocked as the canvas finally fell free.

She was staring into the horrified eyes of the priest. His hands bloody as they clutched at his chest. He tried to speak, but no words came. Instead, he made gasping noises; sucking at air that wouldn't come. Eisen made a stride towards him when she picked up movement to her right. The large man had stepped out from behind a statue and was about to fire. She turned and as she fired, she threw herself down and twisted sideways, hoping it was just enough for his bullet to miss.

As she fell, she fired wildly, squeezing off the remaining five rounds in a desperate attempt to ward off this threat. When she came upon an empty cylinder, time, it seemed for her, froze.

She lay there in the dirt, heart pounding, feeling it in her throat, in her head. She was dead, she was surely dead, she thought. She thought about her daughter, about how she'd see her soon and she realized that she wasn't sad. She didn't feel pain. So this is what it's like, she said quietly to herself. This isn't so bad.

As the adrenaline wore off, Eisen became more aware of her surroundings. The pounding of her heart in her head, in her throat, subsided. She became aware of her breath and realized that she wasn't dying. She felt her head and moved her hands over her torso. She wasn't shot. He had missed.

She slowly raised her head and saw the man, lying on his back thirty feet away. He could have been shot, or he could have been faking it, she thought. After all, he used the priest as a decoy, she reasoned, so perhaps he'd get up and have her at a disadvantage; she carried two extra clips for her automatic, but no speed rounds for her revolver.

She got up quickly now and ran behind the nearest statue. She peeked out and saw that the man had not moved. She moved to the next statue for a better look and now she could see why he lay still. One of her shots caught him in the left eye. The dirt around his head was dark with blood. He wasn't getting up.

She turned her attention to the priest now. She ran over to him and pulled the heavy canvas away from him. The cloth was wet with his blood.

"Shit," she cried as she knelt on the dirt floor in front of the priest.

The priest was very pale and he couldn't move. He rolled his eyes up to Eisen, blood coming from his mouth in spurts and bubbles. He was trying to speak, but couldn't form the words.

"Shhh, don't talk, I'll get you out of here," she said as she slid her arms underneath him. She struggled to pull him up, and when she adjusted her arms around him, she felt a hard object in the priest's waistband. She pulled at it and it came free. It was her service gun. The safety was still on.

She holstered her weapon and tried lifting him again, but to no avail. She tried dragging him by the shoulders, got him closer to the door, but the deep dirt proved a poor surface to get a good grip for her shoes and it made dragging him difficult.

She stopped once more, bent down and got under him and lifted. This time, he seemed to rise with no effort. She looked up and saw another man across from her, supporting the priest. She pulled away and reached for her weapon.

"There is no time," the man said, "If you want to save him, we must hurry."

Chapter 30

Crispis laid the priest upon the bed that Erikson had recently occupied. He had gained sufficient strength to sit up now in an adjacent chair.

Eisen watched as Crispis pulled his shirt open, revealing a large wound in the priest's chest. Blood covered his body and was spilling out onto the bed now.

"He's lost a lot of blood," Crispis said as another man walked slowly to the side of the bed across from Eisen.

"He is near death, Crispis," Judas said.

"You can save him."

"It seems not to matter now."

"You would let him die?"

"Yes."

"But what of your plan?"

"He was the plan."

"We were to keep him safe," Crispis argued, "until the time had come to pass."

"If he dies, that time will never come."

"Please save him," Crispis begged.

"Where is Slava?" Judas asked.

"He's dead. In the basement," Crispis answered.

Judas closed his eyes. He then placed his hands flat and open on the priest's chest so that his fore fingers touched as well as the tips of his thumbs. This left a diamond shaped opening in his hands, framing the wound.

The bleeding stopped. Eisen leaned in closer and saw the flesh ripple like water. She then saw the slug as it worked itself out of the body. She shook her head as she watched the torn flesh come back together as if it were never breached. She thought she might be dreaming as she felt lightness wash over her.

After Judas worked this miracle, he fell back into Crispis' arms. He then turned Judas around and carried him, like a child, from the room. Eisen couldn't move, couldn't feel her limbs. Had what she just witnessed really happened? Had this man appeared and brought this healing upon the priest? She turned to see if her partner had witnessed this same event.

"I tried to tell you," Erikson said as he managed a weak smile.

She turned her attention back to the priest and as she watched him regain his normal breathing, she could once again feel the full weight of her body.

She felt a hand on her right shoulder and though it surprised her, she did not turn suddenly nor feel any danger. She turned her head and saw the man who had helped her carry the priest. He greeted her gaze with a warm smile. She turned her attention back to the priest.

"Did this really just take place," she asked.

"Yes."

"He'll be ok?"

"Like it never happened."

She shook her head in disbelief.

"He healed him?"

"It's what he does," Crispis answered, smiling softly.

Eisen turned back to Crispis and met his smile with one of her own. She then pulled out her gun and pressed it under the man's chin.

"What's your name?"

"There's no need for that now," Crispis said, "we mean you no harm."

"I asked your name," Eisen demanded.

"Crispis."

"Crispis? That's a heavy name. You know what that means don't you?"

"I do."

"And the guy who was just here, the miracle man, who is he?"

"He is Judas."

"He's a Judas? I don't understand."

"No, he is Judas."

"What's his real name?"

"That is his real name."

"This just keeps getting funnier and funnier," Eisen remarked as she pressed her gun harder now under the man's chin, forcing his head back.

"Erikson, keep an eye on the priest. Crispis here is going to introduce me to this Judas."

Crispis paused as he opened the door to a small room where Judas lay. He had felt the pressure of the detective's gun at the back of his neck as they approached the room and now he felt it more sharply as she bade him enter.

"Lights," Eisen commanded.

"That is forbidden," Crispis replied.

"I wasn't asking," Eisen said.

"He cannot have the lights on."

"One last time."

"Then shoot me, for I will bring no further harm to him. He needs time to heal."

"Let's go," she said, pushing him further into the room with her weapon pressed firmly at the base of his skull.

"You do not need that weapon here. We are not a threat."

"So I suppose that large fella was just window dressing?" Eisen asked as she pulled away from Crispis and walked around the bed where Judas lay.

"You provoked him."

Eisen ignored this comment as she walked closer to the prone man. She still held the gun on Crispis, but her full attention now was on this man. He seemed much older than he did just a few minutes ago; his pallor was that of a corpse. She would have thought this man dead were it not for the shallow breath emanating from his lips.

"Wake him."

"I cannot."

Eisen brought her attention back to Crispis and cocked the gun.

"I said, 'wake him.'"

"He is weak; please allow him to rest, in a few hours…"

"I don't have a few hours. Do it now."

"No."

"Excuse me?"

"I will not disturb him. He must rest."

Eisen placed her free hand on the man's shoulder, but he did not move. She shook the man now and found that he still did not wake. She shook him harder now and slapped his face, but he did not respond in the slightest.

"I told you. He must rest, please let him rest."

"Pick him up."

"What?"

"Pick him up. If he needs to rest, he can rest in the car."

"Why are you doing this?"

In an effort to get Crispis moving, she pressed the gun against the prone man's temple, "Let's go, like you did the priest, pick him up and carry him."

Crispis, unsure if Judas was immune to injury while his own body healed, slid his arms underneath the frail man and lifted him off the bed.

"Is there a car?" Eisen asked.

"Yes."

"Can you drive?"

"Yes. It is what I do."

"Let's go."

Crispis felt the barrel against the base of his neck again. He looked up into the rearview mirror and caught Eisen's gaze. He couldn't read her expression and this worried him. He looked over to her right and there laid Judas, slumped over in his seat, just as he had placed him.

"When does he wake up?" Eisen asked.

"It's different every time," he said.

They left the highway and Crispis slowed the vehicle as they came to a red light. He instantly felt the barrel of her gun dig deeper into his neck.

"Uh, uh, don't stop."

"But the light is red," he protested.

"I said don't stop."

Crispis complied, swerving as he missed the lone vehicle at the intersection, fighting to keep the rear of the car square.

"Whenever you come to a red light, you don't stop."

"Fine."

He looked back up in the rearview and he could see tears swelling up in her eyes.

"Are you ok?" Crispis asked.

"Just drive," she answered in a wavering voice.

"You never told me where. Am I still going in the right direction?"

"Seven more blocks," she answered, "then head east a few miles. That's where we're going."

Crispis drove the car in silence. He looked up every few minutes to check on Judas. He could tell by watching his chest that his breathing was becoming more regular. In a few minutes, he guessed, Judas might awaken. Mac was the only one of them that knew how to care for Judas, but now that he was gone, Crispis knew that responsibility would fall to him.

He checked Judas once more in the mirror before slowing the car and turning east. He then looked up again to find Eisen wiping her eyes.

"I'm sorry about your friend," he heard her say.

"Which one?"

"The older one. What was his name?"

"Mac."

"Yes, Mac. I'm sorry about what happened to him."

"Thank you."

"And the other guy, I," she paused, "I've never shot anybody before."

"His name was Slava and, while he wasn't what you might call a good man, he was loyal."

Crispis alternated his eyes between the road ahead and Eisen in the rearview mirror.

"This road," he said, "there's nothing here."

"At the end of the road."

At the road's end Crispis saw a wrought iron archway, flanked by old growth trees. There was no sign, or any indication that what lay beyond the entrance was a cemetery.

The road through the gates rose up, obscuring the vast landscape. As Crispis guided the car over the crest, he was met with acre upon acre of tombstones, crypts and gothic statuary amidst large trees that filled in between every grave. The cemetery looked very beautiful to Crispis and he thought that if this were any other place, it would be considered one of the most beautiful places on earth.

As he eased the car very slowly, he heard Judas begin to stir in the backseat. He stopped the car and turned his attention to Judas.

"Wake him now," Eisen said.

"I don't know how."

"Figure something out," Eisen demanded.

Crispis shut off the engine and went around to the rear passenger door. He opened it and quickly pulled Judas from the seat. He carried him a few yards away to a very large oak tree that cast much shade and sat him up against the massive trunk.

Judas slowly opened his eyes and squinted at the harsh light.

"I'm sorry, Judas," Crispis said, "she has a gun, I was fearful that she would harm you."

Judas strained to focus on Crispis. At first, he seemed disoriented, looking at the man who knelt before him with suspicion. Then recognition came at last and Judas finally smiled.

"Crispis?"

"Yes, Judas?"

"Where are we?"

Crispis turned to look at Eisen, who was standing behind him. While her gun was not trained on them, he found that it was still in her hand.

"Can he walk?" Eisen asked.

"Not yet, I don't think."

"Carry him."

"Where?" Crispis asked.

"Where his services are needed," Eisen replied as she walked ahead, motioning them to follow with her gun.

Crispis carefully pulled Judas up to his feet and placed one arm over his shoulder. They began to walk, with Crispis taking all the weight, for Judas' feet slipped listlessly from side to side.

They followed Eisen across the vast cemetery, taking little notice of the graves of people recently and centuries passed. Crispis tried to carry him under the shade where he could, and pulled Judas close to shield his eyes from the sun when he could not.

At last they came to a fresh plot, where the dirt rose up slightly higher than the ground around it. Crispis stopped several feet away while Eisen continued towards it. He watched as she knelt down by the headstone and said something he could not make out. After a few minutes, she rose and stared at Crispis.

"Bring him here," she said at last.

Crispis carried Judas around the plot, so that they were across the freshly packed earth from where Eisen stood.

"Can he stand?"

Judas patted Crispis gently on the chest and stood on his own. He smiled and nodded to his friend and watched lovingly as Crispis stepped back a few feet.

"How are you?" Eisen asked.

"I am fine."

"Good. Please forgive my forcing you here, but I have a deal for you."

"You have a deal for me?"

"I'm prepared to forget everything, everything I learned about this case, everything I saw, and I mean everything."

"Are you prepared to forget about Mac? What about Slava?" Judas asked.

"What about them?"

"Do they not matter?"

"They are dead by your hands."

"Had it not been for you, they would both be alive," Judas countered.

"I had a job to do."

"And what are you doing now?"

Judas could see Eisen's jaw quiver as she tried to formulate a response. Her eyes filled with tears and as she tried to fight them off, she raised her weapon and leveled it at Judas.

"I want my daughter back," she cried.

"And this is her grave," Judas said.

Eisen nodded her head, the tears beginning to flow.

"I am very sorry for your loss."

Eisen stood firm, waving her gun hand up and down.

"I don't understand what you want," Judas said.

"I want you to bring her back."

Judas wavered a bit in his stance. Crispis stepped forward to help, but he waived him off. He turned to Eisen who was trying to keep her composure.

"Would it be acceptable if I sent Crispis to get some water?"

"No, no help."

"He's not going for help; he'll just go over there," Judas pointed, "not more than thirty yards from here. There's a spigot with a drip can underneath. I can drink from that. You can watch him the whole way, if need be, but he will not run. I only wish to have some water."

Eisen thought about it a minute, eyeing the distance to the spigot, calculating if she had a clear shot before he could make it to the grove of trees twenty yards further on.

"Ok. Hurry."

Crispis set off to gather the drip can and fill it with water. Eisen watched him the whole way, paying little attention to Judas who stepped closer to the headstone.

"She was young," Judas said.

Eisen took her eyes off Crispis and stared at this man for a moment. She could not guess his age, he looked young and at the same time, old.

"She was my everything."

"It hasn't been long, has it?"

"No."

"And you loved her very much."

"With every fiber of my being. She," Eisen paused, "she put little notes in my jacket, barely able to spell with pictures of me and her, some riding ponies together, which we never did, some of us at the beach. Just wonderful things."

Eisen fought hard against the tears.

"I miss her so much," Eisen wailed and collapsed to the ground.

Judas did not move. He did not turn to flee, did not look away nor did he offer any solace. He just stood there and watched her grieve.

Crispis walked quietly to Judas and offered him the water. He took a long drink, and then handed the container back to Crispis. He then knelt down and reached across the grave and touched Eisen gently on the shoulder.

"She is in Heaven now."

"What?"

"She is in God's care now."

"No, that's not what I want," Eisen blurted out through the tears, "I want her back."

"I am very sorry."

Eisen stood up and leveled the gun at Judas' head.

"Bring her back."

"I'm sorry."

"You said that already. Now bring her back!"

"I can't."

"Can't or won't?"

"Does it matter?"

"Did it matter for the priest's child?"

Judas stopped, letting this question sink in. He looked to Crispis, whose eyes were riveted on Eisen.

"What child?" Judas asked, rising.

"The priest's sick child. He doesn't know, does he?" Eisen asked.

"What child? No, that's impossible," Judas began.

"Did you never tell him?"

"That could not happen," Judas said, bewildered now, looking to Crispis, "We got to him. Remember? We got to him before it could happen. We saved him from that fate."

"Before he could fulfill it," Crispis added.

"You knew this would happen?" asked Eisen incredulously.

Judas looked at Eisen and she could feel him looking deep within her.

"I know of vague things, prophecies foretold many centuries ago. I knew of a priest, of this time and place, a priest destined for greatness, destined to usher in a new age of the church. This man would bring the fractured together, unite the divisions into one. He would make us believe again. However, it was also foretold of a woman that would tempt him, could bare his child and this act, this one simple act would destroy him and the world would never experience what it truly means to love. "

"Then, out of this love," Eisen began, "Please give me back my daughter."

"I told you, I cannot. Once the soul leaves the body, once the heart is silent, there is nothing I can do. I cannot heal the body without the soul."

"Try," Eisen said.

"No."

"Last chance," Eisen said as she aimed her weapon on Judas's chest.

Judas looked at Eisen for what seemed to her like an eternity before he lowered his head and whispered 'I'm sorry, but I cannot.'

The first shell exploded in a deafening roar as the bullet left Eisen's gun and ripped though Judas' heart. The force of the slug knocked Judas back a step. He looked down at the wounds, then up at Eisen without a hint of emotion on his face.

Eisen emptied her clip, firing round after round into Judas from point blank range. As the last round tore yet another hole through him, he staggered back and fell. Blood flowed freely from his wounds. Crispis ran to Judas and tried to help him up, but Judas motioned with his hand for him to step away.

Eisen watched in disbelief as the man she had shot numerous times in the heart, slowly rose to his feet. The blood had ceased to flow and through the tattered shirt, she could see the bullets that had not passed through him, work their way out one by one and fall to the ground.

"I have tried, Detective Eisen," Judas began, "I have tried a great many times in almost every conceivable manner. Nothing works. I am a man condemned to walk the earth this way until the end of days or until our God sees fit and there is nothing you or I can do to stop it."

"Believe me," he continued, "if I could bring your child back to you, I would. I know the depth of your despair and can feel the weight it bears upon you and for that, I am truly sorry."

Eisen stood there not knowing what to say, not knowing if what she just witnessed actually took place. She shot a man multiple times, and he rose as if she never fired a shot.

She stepped backwards from Judas, shaking her head, her mouth struggling against words that would not come.

"No, no, no, no.," she finally screamed, tripping on an adjacent headstone and fell, her gaze not leaving Judas. She stared at him until she got up, then she turned and ran off, leaving Judas and Crispis at her daughter's grave.

Chapter 31

When Judas and Crispis made it back to the warehouse, they found Detective Erikson, sitting on a chair, trying to remove the strips of luxurious cloth. Father Donovan, lying next to him on the bed, was repeating the Lord's Prayer like a mantra and didn't pay the two any mind as they entered.

When the priest finally stopped praying, he looked up to face Judas, who stood motionless before him.

"Crispis," Judas began, "please remove the bandages from the detective. He no longer needs them."

"You never told me about Slava," Donovan interrupted.

"His story wasn't mine to tell."

"How did you find him?"

"He was hanged."

"But he wasn't dead."

"No. He lasted on that noose for a very long time. I knew then that there was something special about his soul."

"He was a monster."

"Nobody is a monster."

"He killed people."

"Nobody is a saint, either."

"He enjoyed it."

"Donovan," Judas began, "if you were given the chance to save a soul, would you save it?"

"If I had known…"

"No, no preconditions, would you save it?"

Donovan turned towards Crispis, who was busy removing the strips of cloth from the detective. He then looked back at Judas, and then looked down at his hands, still folded in prayer.

"Yes I would," he said finally.

"Thank you."

"But you knew."

"Yes."

"But you still…"

"It matters not. What if I had told you that those he killed deserved such a punishment? What if those who died at his hands inflicted such cruelty upon those undeserving of it? What then, father? Would you judge him as harshly?"

"You know I wouldn't."

"Then it matters not if he killed for pleasure or retribution. Taking a life is taking a life, be it for good or ill."

Judas offered Donovan a kindly smile.

"Do you really wish to understand my selection of Slava?"

"Yes."

"His was much like yours."

"How so?"

"You and he travelled similar paths."

"I doubt that."

"It's true. In fact, the two of you were much alike."

"How can someone who murders people be like someone who follows the path of God?"

"You'd be surprised how many times in human history those traits are intertwined."

"Are you saying I'm capable of murder?" Donovan asked incredulously, rising now from the bed.

"No."

"Then what are you saying?"

"The two of you shared such a passion for God and as such, a belief in salvation."

"He had a funny way of showing it."

"People show their love for God in many different ways and people interpret his teachings differently. Ways that seems oppositional to the beliefs of others are no less valid."

"Perhaps they're just wrong. Did he not tread in the face of God's teachings?"

"His teachings are for introspection, for guidance. They are not law."

"They are his word," Donovan challenged.

"What do you know of his word? You know only of what was written down, the mortal understandings of His word interpreted by idiots. Tell me, who was qualified to carry on the words of God? Who was good enough? Did they not take it upon themselves, put themselves above others, and even saint themselves? Such arrogance despite His teachings!"

"They were your friends."

"They were fools. I was the one he trusted," Judas roared. "I was the one who sacrificed and for what? Hmm? I was the one who was forsaken while those with lesser love stole the glory of God."

"I don't think God would look at it that way."

"Really? Tell me, what do you know of it? You've only learned from what they have laid out for you. I was there."

"I don't think I want to talk to you about this anymore."

"You don't want to know then?"

"No."

"I was saving you."

"Saving me from what?"

"From him."

"'Him?' Him who? Speak plainly!"

Judas went to Erikson and took the last strip of cloth Crispis had unwound. He held it up to Donovan.

"This cloth, while beautiful, is merely a cloth. What makes it special is its purpose."

He grabbed more of the strips Crispis had removed from Erikson and held them up to Donovan.

"There are many priests, many worthy, and like this cloth, meaningless until they are called for a common purpose. These strips of cloth are nothing more than tools for a higher purpose. Yet even a single strip of cloth has such potential, just as one priest alone has, but it must be enacted upon and not discarded."

"What are you getting at?"

"There are many gospels not included in the bible. One such gospel foretells of a man that will usher in a new age, an epoch of such beauty and love. Can you imagine; no wars, no hatred, only beauty and love? Can you?"

231

"Of course," Donovan replied, "that man is Jesus at the rapture."

"No, that man is you."

"Judas, I followed you because I had lost my faith and I saw in you a connection to God. I saw a great many things, things only Jesus himself could do. And now I see you as delusional, perhaps even mad."

"Would you find me mad if I were to tell you, that I believed unlike I've ever believed before that you were to be the one to usher in this golden age?"

"I am but a simple priest."

"You had a great future."

"Had?"

"It is also foretold that you would be tempted."

"By whom?" By the devil?"

"There is no devil, only the choices we make."

"What is this temptation?"

"A woman."

Donovan moved his mouth, formed words with his lips, yet no sound came out. He looked pale, his hands began to shake and his head fell heavily back onto the bed.

"Is this true?" Judas asked.

"There is a woman, yes, whom I loved, still love."

"Is there a child?"

"What?" Donovan asked.

He looked to Judas, expecting condemnation, but found no such judgment.

"Detective Eisen spoke of a child," Judas continued, "a female child."

"Eisen," Erikson interrupted, "where is she?"

"I do not know. However, if I had to guess, I would say that given her emotional state, she would be at the one place in which she finds solace."

Erikson kicked off the rest of the strips of cloth and rose from the chair.

"How are you feeling?" Judas asked.

"Fine, now. I must go."

"Will you be arresting us, Detective?" Crispis asked.

Erikson looked at the man before him, tried to piece together the happenings of the past day in a memory that registered no such detail. He then shook his head.

"Your weapon is on the bedside table. Take it and go."

As Erikson left, Judas walked past Donovan, but was stopped by the priest's hand.

"Where is she?" he asked.

"The woman?"

"The child."

Judas looked down upon Donovan, noted the tears swelling in his eyes and smiled lovingly at him.

"She is where all children are who are nearest to God."

Chapter 32

Judas zipped the large duffel bag closed and handed it, with some effort, to Crispis.

"There's three million in cash. Do with it whatever you will."

"I don't need this much," Crispis protested.

"Who else is there to give it to?"

"You could donate it like we've donated everything else."

"This was saved for those that followed me, to provide for them in the event anything happened to me," Judas replied. "Three followers, three million, each getting a million. You are the only one left, so you get it all."

"I will do good with this," Crispis said.

"I know you will," Judas said, then paused. "When you leave here, when you are no longer with with me, after a time you will begin to age again."

"I'm actually looking forward to it."

Judas smiled, something that Crispis realized he had rarely seen him do.

"Where will you go?" Judas asked.

"I don't know yet. You have provided me with the only home I can remember. You, Slava and Mac are my only family."

"You can start a new family. After all, you are still young."

"I'll miss you," Crispis said, voice wavering.

He stepped forward and took Judas in his arms for a brief moment, then pulled away.

Crispis turned to leave then stopped. He turned back to Judas, his eyes rimmed with tears.

"I'm sorry, Judas, if I failed you."

"It is I that have failed, Crispis, not you. I failed to prevent Father Donovan from suffering a fate similar to mine. I saw a means to right the wrongs done unto me, yet my actions, it seems, were not swift enough."

Crispis nodded his head solemnly.

"Go now," Judas said at last, "and never come back to this place."

After Crispis left, Judas made haste and dragged Mac to the basement level where Slava lay. He dug two graves and laid their bodies to rest. He then gave them last rites, spoke a few kind words of them aloud to no one and went back upstairs.

Judas could immediately smell smoke. He inhaled deeply and smiled as he exhaled.

"Gauloises."

"You always had a good nose," Jesus said.

"I could always appreciate a good French cigarette."

"And their wine," Jesus added.

"No. You made the best wine."

"Shall we?"

"No, Jesus. I won't let you have him."

Jesus laughed and shook his head as if the enormity of the joke was beyond Judas' understanding.

"My dear friend, have you thought all this time it was about him? It was never about him. He fulfilled his destiny before you were able to get your hands on him and hide him away from me. Your sequestering of the most important man, at least the most instrumental man, in the history of your alternate new dawn, was for naught."

"Then why are you here?"

"My dear friend, I am here for you."

"You're wasting your time then."

"Am I? Hmmm, then perhaps I came back at the wrong point in history. You do realize that the time has come for me to return and usher in a new era of peace and love."

"The new era of peace and love will not come. You have made sure of that."

"We shall see. Come, let's go."

"What will become of Crispis? How will you judge him?"

"I will offer him absolution."

"What about the priest?"

"What of him?"

"What will be his path now?"

"That is up to him."

"Will he be forgiven?"

"My dear Judas, at the end of days, is forgiveness really all you would think about?"

"Yes."

"All they really need, including our young priest here, or you, will ever need, is my understanding and love."

"You know, I think I liked you better in the garden. At least then, I didn't suspect you were up to something."

Jesus laughed as he walked to the door and opened it. He gestured for Judas follow. Judas walked to the door then stopped at the threshold and looked back at his room.

"Will I need anything?"

"Everything has been taken care of."

Judas smiled and shook his head.

"No drama, then?"

"I think the less of it now the better. Don't you agree, Judas?"

"It's your show."

"Shall we then?"

"May I have one of those cigarettes?"

"Certainly."

Jesus produced the packet and shook it, causing a few think sticks to emerge. Judas selected one, placed it between his lips and nodded when Jesus had provided enough fire. He inhaled deeply, held it for a moment, and then exhaled, nodding his head as if in agreement.

"Mmm," Judas purred.

"It's been awhile."

"Yes, it has," Judas agreed.

"Funny, isn't it, how things turn out?"

"Was it funny to you then, in the garden? Did you understand how this would all play out?"

"To a point."

"Then why do you still need me?"

"You shall see."

"Speak plainly," Judas demanded, exhaling a plume of white smoke, "I think the occasion deserves it."

237

"It would be easier to show you. Will you come with me, now? All will be revealed and you will understand at long last why things had to be as they are."

"May I finish my cigarette?"

"Of course."

When Judas exhaled the last breath of smoke, Jesus spit into his palm and rubbed his hands together. He then placed his moist palms upon the eyes of Judas and massaged them. The room instantly began to blur and Judas felt a sense of calm and well-being such that he had not felt in so long. Peace was returning to him. He felt light, felt an energy that was both uplifting and joyous. Then calm passed to confusion and he became delirious. The light faded. Sound ceased. He lurched forward, breaking Jesus' grasp on him and sprawled out on the floor, struggling for breath. Then the darkness took him.

He didn't know when he first heard the buzzing noise, but he felt it deep within his brain. He opened his eyes and realized he was in a different place. The air smelled different, the mood of the room felt different. The lighting was different. It was darker here, quieter. The noises didn't echo like he had expected.

Once the buzzing he felt grew softer, he managed to stand up. With some effort, he brought his eyes into focus. He was surrounded by several bassinets, one in particular whose occupant was hooked up to machines that beeped and clicked and monitored the heartbeat.

"This is a special place," he heard Jesus say behind him.

He sat up, turned and saw Jesus leaning into the bassinet, smiling.

"I thought you were, that we were…," Judas began.

"In heaven?"

"Yes. I thought…"

"That it's over?"

"Isn't it?"

"Not quite."

"Then where are we?"

"The most desperate prayers for my help come from places such as this. No prayer is as beautiful as one that begs for the life of a child."

"How long have we been here?" Judas asked, rubbing his eyes.

"A few hours."

"I've been laying here that long?"

"Yes."

"And nobody here seemed to notice? I find that odd."

"They cannot see us," Jesus answered.

Judas rose, approached Jesus and looked into the bassinet he was staring into. There lay an infant. Judas stepped back and looked into the next bassinet. Then the next, not stopping until he had inspected all the bassinets. He found all the others to be empty.

"Where are we?" Judas asked.

"Where you were always destined to be."

"And where is that?"

"At the end of the world."

Chapter 33

Donovan's thoughts consumed him. He knew where he had to be, but his mind was preoccupied with thoughts and memories. What led him here? Why had he become a priest in the first place? If one is to question one's calling, he surmised, one might as well start at the beginning.

He concluded that he could not put any blame upon the young woman, Patricia, whose mere presence had caused him to waver. Perhaps she was a test. God was testing me. Did I fail, though? Was becoming a priest really my calling?

But why did he develop these feeling for this woman? And why did they still remain? He had not seen her in many months, but still he felt his heart longing for her.

I used to dream about becoming Pope, he thought as he smiled silently. And why not? Why could there not be

an American Pope? I had a great start, a promising future.
Why not me? But then again, why did he feel he was above
such a test? Perhaps he was destined for a situation such as
this to test his quality. Who was I to think myself above
such events?

He walked along silently for another few miles,
gazing absentmindedly at the buildings, at the businesses
occupying the storefronts and the people working within
without letting the cityscape engage him.

His body on autopilot, his way-finding was directed
by habit. His thoughts finally gave way to the present when
he realized where his body had stopped and refused to go
further. It took a few minutes to recognize, for his eyes to
come into focus and understand where he was.

He had come to a stop outside the coffee shop where
he had first spoken to Patricia, first gotten to hear her voice,
watch her eyes move as she spoke.

"Well, if this isn't a perfect book-end moment to
things," he joked, speaking his mind aloud.

The shop was closed, he could see, but it wasn't off-
limits to his imagination. He pictured her here again, sitting
with him, before this all started. He asked himself a simple
question as he let her voice play in his mind: could I stop it if
I had it to do all over again?

No, he couldn't. He knew his answer now, he knew
his path. He knew he was still with God, despite following
Judas, whom he had given his service to these dark months.

And what of Judas? Was he truly who he claimed to
be? Did he claim such great things that most in his self-
appointed status claim? No, he did not. Did he take
advantage of the weak-minded? No, he did not. He seemed
to avoid such ties. He avoided entitlements despite being
someone who claimed such special consul with God.

And did he not have a gift? Would God give such a gift to someone unworthy? No such man who claimed himself above others, no man who put himself next to God was special. They were just men, mortal men who suffered from great ills: greed, power, lust. But, this one was different. This one did not want the role that God had given him.

Was he truly who he had claimed to be?

Was he really immortal?

Who was he really?

And why did he choose me?

Why did she choose me?

Why did I fall in love with her?

He chased these thoughts by returning to her. He could see her again now, in the coffee shop, standing there. He reached his hand and pressed it against the glass, imagining that he could touch her, feel her warmth. He closed his eyes and pretended she was with him again.

He as so deep in thought that he did not hear the cab pull up behind him, nor did he hear the door open and the passenger step out.

"Hello," he heard a voice say.

He opened his eyes and turned around and found her standing before him.

"Patricia, I," he stammered.

He tried to think of something to say, something that could explain his absence, why he left so abruptly, but he couldn't find any.

"I'm so sorry," he began.

"It's ok. I need you to come with me," she said, almost aware of his thoughts, "I have someone I want you to meet."

"We have a child."

"Yes, but please, we don't have much time," she said, this time with a more desperate tone in her voice.

Chapter 34

Erikson took the stairs three at a time, as he hurried to Eisen's apartment. When he got to the door he knocked softly and called her name. After the third time with no answer, he tried the knob. It was unlocked.

He opened the door and stepped inside. He noticed her jacket on the floor. On the kitchen counter, he saw her keys next to a bottle opener with the cork still embedded in it. He looked towards the hallway leading to her bedroom and saw light coming from her daughter's bedroom.

He approached quietly, listening for sounds. He heard someone crying. He knew that she didn't hear him approach, so he made some noise with his feet before knocking softly at the door.

"Deb?"

There was no answer. He opened the door slowly and peered into the room. There he found his partner, Detective Deborah Eisen, sitting on the bed of her deceased child, a wine glass in one hand and her service issue 9mm in the other. A bottle of wine was on the floor by her right foot.

"Deb," he called as he breached the threshold, "may I come in?"

Eisen looked up at him and said nothing. She looked away and took a sip of wine. Erikson took another step into the room and closed the door behind him.

"Deb, I'm here for you Deb," he said as he walked slowly to a small chair across the room from where Eisen was and sat down.

"Deb, do me a favor, put your gun away."

Eisen, still fixated on something very far away, nodded her head very slowly, as if trying to understand something. She ignored Erikson's request.

"Deb," he tried again, "do you think I can have some of that wine?"

After getting no answer, Erikson knelt on the floor and reached out and took the bottle of wine in his hand and sat back in the chair with it. He took a drink, keeping his eyes on his partner.

"Deb," he tried again, "I know this has been one fucked up day, with a lot of shit happening that we can't explain. But I need you to talk to me."

She brought the glass to her lips and held it there as she finished it. She then dropped it onto the bed, where it rolled off and smashed onto the floor.

"Deb," Erikson began again, but stopped as he saw Eisen finally acknowledge his presence.

"I took him."

"Who?"

"The guy that saved your life. I took him with me to see my daughter. I wanted him to bring her back, like he did to you and the young priest, like he did to those other children. But he refused."

"Deb, I…"

"So I shot him. I shot him and kept shooting him, but he got up. How fucked up is that?"

"I know Deb, I know."

"Do you? Do you really? Do you have any idea how I feel right now?"

"I can't imagine how you feel."

"I can't either. That's just it; I can't feel anything but the pain. I am so empty right now. I tried to do the right thing. I tried to bring her back. I thought he could do it. He saved so many others. Why couldn't he save my little girl?"

"I don't know, Deb."

Eisen smiled at Erikson and wiped some of the tears from her face.

"I'm glad you came, Mark, it was good to see you one last time."

"Deb, don't do this."

"I'll have to kindly ask you to leave now."

"No, I'm not leaving you."

"Please, for me, just grant me this one kindness."

"I'll go if you surrender your weapon."

"That's not gonna happen."

He saw that she was no longer smiling. She took a deep breath and brought the 9mm up and pressed the barrel firmly against her chest.

"This is where the pain is," she said. "I just want it to stop."

"Deb, don't. Deb, look at me," he screamed as he leapt from the chair.

Erikson made it only halfway between them when she pulled the trigger.

Chapter 35

"Showtime," Jesus said as he snapped his fingers and almost as if on cue, Judas saw Donovan and Patricia enter the Neonatal Intensive Care Unit.

"Shhh," scolded Judas.

"They cannot hear us. It's as if we are not here."

"Then make it as if we truly are not here."

"I'm afraid you must be here."

"And why is that?"

"The prophecy must be fulfilled."

"It was fulfilled. You got what you wanted."

"Not quite."

"What else, then?"

Jesus smiled in response, allowing Judas to beg the question, which he ignored.

"My return," Jesus continued.

"You are here, so do what needs to be done."

"Me? This is your moment."

"What do you mean?"

"You will see. The show is about to start."

Judas watched as the young couple approached the bassinet in which the infant lay. He could not hear what they were saying.

He watched as Donovan took the woman's hand into his. They smiled at each other for a moment, and then she took his hand and guided it towards the child. Donovan gently placed his hand upon the head of the infant. It did not move in response.

"What are they doing?" Judas asked.

"I believe they are saying goodbye."

Judas watched as the young woman picked the infant up and held her in her arms. He could see that she gave Donovan a smile that held no malice, then handed him the child. He took the child into his arms and held her close. He then bent down and placed a kiss upon her forehead.

The woman put her arms around the priest and held them both in an embrace. For an instant, Judas thought, they could be any family.

He watched silently as they held each other. He watched as Donovan's shoulders began to move up and down as he wept. He watched and he knew they were experiencing pain; a pain he himself had experienced many, many years ago.

A nurse appeared a few moments later and after a brief conversation, they laid the infant back down in the bassinet and followed her out of the ward.

"Where are they going?" Judas asked.

"To make arrangements."

"So that's it?"

Judas turned to Jesus, but he did not respond.

"Let us go, then," Judas said.

"Go?"

"Yes."

"Where?"

"Anywhere."

"But my dear, Judas, there is nowhere else. This is where you were always meant to be. This is your destiny."

"My destiny was to save the priest, to keep him from you, but I have failed. There is nothing else."

"You believe you have failed at your task when the truth is that you have yet to have had your opportunity."

Jesus ushered Judas to the bassinet.

"This," he continued, whispering into his ear "is your destiny."

Judas stared at the infant.

"This is my vessel," Jesus continued.

"It is the means of my second coming," he added.

"Will you not save me?"

Judas stepped away from the bassinet. He could feel his heartbeat in his throat, his head pounding. He turned towards Jesus and without taking his eyes off the dying infant, shook his head.

"No."

"You will not save me?"

"This," Judas began, "this is why you have brought me here? This is why you have made me roam the earth these two thousand years? For this one moment, I've had to endure so much pain and torment?"

"Yes."

"Why could you not tell me this? In the garden, when you kissed me, why could you not make plain that this was your plan?"

"It is my way."

"This is why I could not take my life?"

"Yes."

"And this is why I was left to wander the earth?"

"Yes."

"Why did you do this to me?"

"You were worthy. You gave up everything so that I could be sacrificed for the sins of the world. Who else could I ask?"

"But you didn't ask."

"Yes."

"You left me. You abandoned me."

"You were never alone."

"You forsook me! That night, alone in the fields when my blood would not flow; where was my savior? I was left asunder, put out of your love! I spoke to you, prayed to you, but never once did you answer."

Jesus said nothing in response. He merely placed a loving hand upon Judas' shoulder, which was quickly brushed away.

"Were you testing me?"

Jesus only smiled at him.

"Could you have warned me? Sent me a sign? Had I known that I would have to endure for these many years for you, I would have gladly done it. I did as you asked once, out of my love for you. Does that love not get returned? Do I not count as worthy? Look at all I have done for you, Jesus. Why do you not place me in your favor?"

"But I do. You above all others."

"You do not."

"You do not believe me?"

"No, I do not, not anymore. There was a time when you could have reached me and I would have done anything you asked, as I once did. But after I was cast out, after I was

251

erased from all your teachings, after my name was made akin to betrayal, after many years, my heart became dark."

Judas turned his attention back to the bassinet. Jesus walked closer to Judas and whispered in his ear.

"She is not much older than your child," he said.

"Do not speak to me of my child."

"You can save her."

"You have the power, so you do it yourself," Judas replied.

"I cannot. I have been born again unto this child's body. She is my vessel. It is up to you."

Judas reached a hand into the bassinet and placed it softly on the child's head.

"This is you?"

"Yes," Jesus whispered softly. "She is the manner of my return."

"I cannot recall my son's face," Judas said. "I remember watching him as he drew his last breath; afraid to hold him for fear that my curse would bar him from the Kingdom of Heaven. Yet for all my love for him, I can no longer recall his face."

"He was beautiful."

"I miss him. I've missed him every day. Why did you take him, Jesus? Why couldn't you have afforded me that one happiness?"

"Judas, when your child died, I took his spirit up in my arms and held him. I wanted to feel something that was a part of you. I could feel the love you put into your child. The love for your child is still strong, and as you still love him, I know you still love me."

"I've stopped loving you."

"You'll not do this for me?"

"I will not."

"Then for your child."

"It's a funny thing," Judas said as he turned to face Jesus, "you made me immortal but I never stopped being human. And while I was immune to the ills of the body, I was never immune to the ills of the mind. I have gown wise, certainly, but I have never let go of my anger towards you. You give me a gift, a gift I could have used to save my child, yet I was unaware that I possessed this gift. And only after he dies do I learn that I have this power. And though I have saved many, I could not save the one who could have made the difference. Though I have in my body this ability to heal, I do not hold in my heart the willingness to forgive."

Jesus smiled and walked away from the bassinet towards the window. Lights, alternating red and white were penetrating the blinds. He pushed them aside and peered out.

"Such a shame," Jesus said.

Judas turned to face him, but did not speak.

"Detective Eisen," Jesus coaxed, "it's really such a shame."

"What about her?" Judas asked.

"She shot herself. You didn't know that? Of course you didn't, how could you? The paramedics are wheeling her in right now. It doesn't look good."

"Why do you tell me this?"

"I thought you might care."

"I do not."

"She is dying, Judas. It would be such a shame to have her soul be denied eternity with her daughter."

"Then you go save her."

"Wouldn't it be nice if I did? Yes, it would. But I'd have to save two lives, not just one. I'd be saving her partner's life as well. He loves her, did you know that? Such a passion he has for her. Who knows, maybe they'll have a life together. He might even give her a child; a second chance so to speak."

"Where's my second chance?"

"It's right here."

"It's too late, Jesus. I decided long ago that I would no longer follow you. You took too long and offered me too little. You offer me nothing now."

"I offer you everything."

"Then go. Leave me."

"Very well, then. I will be downstairs in the ER, watching over Detective Eisen. Her fate will be decided by you."

"Do not put this upon me."

"My dear Judas, you have put this upon yourself by following me, by loving me and ultimately by turning away from me. Don't you see? It was always up to you."

Judas watched as Jesus disappeared; his visage became like a ghost, then nothing more. He then turned his attention back to the bassinet. He reached down and pulled free the wires that sustained her life. He then shut off the alarms and stared at the infant.

"If you are to die," he said at last, "you will not be left alone to die in this crib."

He placed his hands gently under the infant and pulled her from the bassinet.

He looked at her and found he was no longer looking at a baby girl in a pink cap, warmed in a cotton wrap, but a boy, naked, swaddled in a woolen blanket. He was starring into the eyes of his son. He looked up and saw only darkness. The room in which he had been standing was gone. Nothing existed outside the embrace of his child. As Jesus had foretold, he was truly at the end of the world.

He pulled the child closer. As he leaned down, the child cooed and opened his eyes. He knew in his heart that his son was smiling at him.

"My son! My beautiful baby boy! Oh how I have longed to hold you in my arms," Judas cooed. "To hear your soft breath and to know that you feel warmth and happiness when I am holding you comforts me greatly. There is so much I wanted from this. To watch you grow, to see you become the man I always knew you'd become: righteous and true. I wish we had more time. I wish you could have known me. I wish you could understand the love I have carried in my heart for you these endless years. I have never, ever stopped loving you."

"But you are dead, and we never had a moment like this. How I have wished for a time when I saw hope, when I could look into your eyes and see a purpose for my sacrifice and know that I could be whole again. But you are dead and I never knew you or the happiness you could bring. I have known only sorrow and pain."

His son just looked at him. He did not offer Judas solace or absolution. He did not pass judgment. He merely offered him love.

Judas closed his eyes. He was memorizing his son's face so that he would never forget it again. He felt warmth he had never experienced before wash over him and as it finally began to fade, he opened his eyes. His son was gone. Judas found himself sitting on the floor of the hospital room with the baby girl in his lap.

Judas felt the infant's breath become labored. He knew that all he had to do was to pull her close, hold her tight and she would be healed.

He began to pull her close, and then stopped. The infant, on the verge of death, lay quite still; her life and her future in his hands. He felt the weight of her upon him, the

255

weight of everything now, every life and every soul, bearing down on him. Save her now, he could hear Jesus say, and all will be forgiven. Save her and you will be saved. But he found that now, in the moment of truth, where all is laid bare, his salvation no longer mattered.

He could only think of his son.

No sound came from outside the room. The sense of serenity was so strong now, that he no longer felt his own heart beat. He tried again to pull her close, to hold her, but he began to tremble. He bent forward to kiss the infant, and as he gently placed his lips upon her hers, he began to weep.